"will be if I'm thin?

I could hardly bear the thought of losing Brad, but then I couldn't keep him either, not when he was nagging me the way he had. What Naomi said about some boys not wanting their girlfriends to be too attractive flashed through my mind, but it wasn't that. It was just him panicking because his sister had had anorexia. It was crazy really, because if he saw how fat I was, he'd go off me anyway.

I thought about it all the way home. Without him, I could diet properly, I'd have a real chance to lose my fat.

The train wheels clattered rhythmically. *Ta ta ta, tattata ta!* Just like the mantra that wound around my head:

He *will* love me when I'm thin. Everything will be perfect then.

I Slept With My Best Friend's Boyfriend
Sue Dando

My Sister – The Superbitch
Rosie Corrigan

My Boyfriend's Older Than My Dad
Jill Eckersley

They Think I'm Too Easy
Lorna Read

I Taught Him a Lesson He'll Never Forget
Amber Vane

"will he love me if I'm thin?"

Kirsty White

■SCHOLASTIC

Scholastic Children's Books
Commonwealth House, 1–19 New Oxford Street,
London WC1A 1NU, UK
A division of Scholastic Ltd
London ~ New York ~ Toronto ~ Sydney ~ Auckland
Mexico City ~ New Delhi ~ Hong Kong

First published in the UK by Scholastic Ltd, 1998

Copyright © Kirsty White, 1998

ISBN 0 590 11346 1

Typeset by Falcon Oast Graphic Art
Printed by Cox and Wyman Ltd, Reading, Berks.

10 9 8 7 6 5 4 3 2 1

Prologue

I don't know when it began or why. I do know that for a long time I blamed it on Brad, my boyfriend. We'd been together for a while, but not so long that we'd begun to take each other for granted. It was my first serious relationship; I'd been crazy about Brad for ages, and so had my best friend, Naomi. In fact, Naomi and I had fallen out when I started going out with him. Naomi's absolutely gorgeous whereas I'm rather plain, and I don't think that she could cope with the fact that he liked me more than her.

I felt pretty insecure about Brad. I kept on wondering what he saw in me. Often, when I looked at other girls, or even when I thought about them, I'd feel certain that sooner or later Brad would be bound to leave me and go off with someone else. I never said anything to him, though; I was afraid that I'd give him the wrong idea.

I was insecure about everything back then. I'm the baby of the family; my sister Maddie is two years older than me, and I felt that I went through life under her shadow. Our parents are the archetypical over-achievers: my father's a lawyer with his own firm and my mother's the personnel director of a big computer company. Madds looks set to follow effortlessly in their footsteps; she's brilliant, beautiful, witty and wise, whereas for me everything is a bit of a struggle.

I was getting good grades at school, but I had to work hard to get them. I didn't think I'd be able to match Maddie's four A-grade A levels, or get on to the course in Law and European Studies that she's doing.

We live in this beautiful house filled with brilliant people and I used to think that the odd one out was me. I felt clumsy and stupid compared to the rest of the family. I'd imagine people saying, 'It's such a pity about Jo.'

I just didn't live up to the family ideal. I was afraid that sooner or later everybody, especially my parents, would discover the truth about me. And then they just wouldn't care any more.

I couldn't meet the high expectations they had. I, Jo Gibson, was an imposter, the odd one out.

The worst thing was, I was fat. Not exactly gross, but

there was a layer of lard around my tummy and my thighs. I'd always been well built – I guess that's the best way of putting it – but at Christmas the year before, I'd really piled it on. I remember not being able to get into my favourite jeans afterwards and the weight just wouldn't go away.

I always meant to do something about it but I wasn't too bothered until I met Brad. Everybody fancied him, you see, and I was really paranoid that he'd leave me for someone else. I just couldn't see what he saw in me; every time I looked in the mirror, I was disgusted with myself. I kept on trying to lose weight; I'd give up chocolate or cheese, but it only ever lasted for a day or two.

No matter what I did, the weight stayed on.

I decided that had to change when I fell in love.

Chapter 1

One day sticks in my mind. It was late May, the beginning of summer. We couldn't spend much time together because although I'd finished my exams, Brad, who's a year older than me, was in the middle of his A Levels, but we used to meet up in the afternoon for a couple of hours. That day we were walking through town and I was glancing in shop windows, checking my reflection and thinking, as always, how gross I looked.

"You're gorgeous," Brad insisted.

I looked away. He was always saying things like that, although I knew that he was just trying to be kind to me.

"No, I'm not," I said. "I'm plain, and my hair's a mess." I was going to say that my breasts were too small and my hips were too big, but I stopped. I didn't want to draw his attention to it.

"Your hair's great and you're about as plain as Dory Lyon," Brad said.

I gaped at him. Dory Lyon was a couple of years older than me. When she left school she went down to London to stay with her sister. She said she was going to try modelling but nobody thought she would make it, although she'd always been the local drop-dead gorgeous, look-at-me-and-die girl. We didn't hear anything for a couple of months and everybody was beginning to bitch, then Dory got taken on by a top model agency. Now she's the new supermodel, making a zillion pounds an hour and commuting to New York by Concorde. There's a picture of her in the papers nearly every day. In the local paper, there's a picture of her every *single* day!

"That's not even funny," I said, folding my arms over the pathetic pimples that are supposed to be my breasts.

"It's not meant to be, Jo," Brad said. "You should look in a mirror sometime. You're really something, you know?"

I groaned. Looking in mirrors is something that I do a lot of. "You're prejudiced," I said. "You're my boyfriend."

"Yes, but I always thought you were great looking, even before we started going out."

I groaned again. Everybody said I was lucky to have Brad, but sometimes I wondered if I'd be better with a boyfriend who told the truth.

We took the bus home and Brad walked me to my door. "You know," he said, "you should send your picture in for that roadshow. . ."

"Brad!" I pushed him playfully. There was one of these TV roadshows coming to town and they'd advertised for people to model for them. Dory Lyon was going to be the star attraction, if she had a moment to spare between flying to the fashion capitals of the world.

Brad staggered as if I'd really hurt him, then he came close to kiss my cheek.

"You really should, Jo," he said.

I folded my arms over my burgeoning stomach. "I haven't exactly got a model figure."

"Ah, but fashion's changing at last," he persisted. "They don't want waifs any more. They want real people. People like you."

He kissed my cheek again and then he left.

"I feel like an elephant," I grumbled under my breath, as I watched him walk away with that loose, confident stride of his.

Brad wants to be a commercial pilot; it's one of these one-in-ten-thousand chances but he's prepared to try and I respect him for that. He's going to apply for the British Airways training scheme and, if that fails, he's going to become a flight engineer.

Me, I wouldn't even have the courage to fill in the application form! I do well at school because I'm a closet swot. When everybody else is watching the late-night movie I'm burning the midnight oil with my schoolbooks. I'm always afraid that people will discover the truth about me, which is that I'm dumb.

When I got in, Gran had dinner ready. Because my parents both work, she came to help care for us when we were little and, now that we're older, she's still around. Gran believes in what she calls good, wholesome food: three square meals a day, lots of vegetables and also stodge because she says you need plenty of energy when you're growing up. Her eyesight's not too hot – she can't see just how much I've already grown up.

She stands over you as you're eating, and if you don't finish your greens then you don't get pudding.

She calls it healthy food, but it'd only be healthy for starving Rwandans! I'd rather have salads and rice, but she'd have a fit if I told her that.

As soon as I got in, she plonked down a plate of steak pie and potatoes and carrots and beans. I began to eat mechanically, but I wasn't hungry. I was thinking of what Brad had said about Dory Lyon, and wondering what my life would be like if I was as slim as her.

"Come on," Gran said, "there's apple pie for afters."

Although I adore Gran's apple pie, I thought fleetingly that maybe I shouldn't eat it, because all that sugar would just add more weight to my hips.

I didn't see Brad for a few days after that; he had to swot for his maths exam. After school I ambled round town, vaguely looking for a job. My father had said that I could help out in his office, making tea and so on, but I wanted something more exciting than that – and something that would make a bit more money. Brad had managed to get a job as a summer relief porter at the hospital and it paid really well. We'd talked about going away to Spain with some friends in August once he'd got his exam results.

Even thinking about the results made me shake; Brad needed really good grades and I was afraid that he wouldn't make it. He acted like he didn't care but, deep down, I knew that he was worried. He said that he could take it if he failed the flying aptitude tests, but he'd be really cut up if he flunked just because he'd dropped a grade in one of his exams.

I was worried too, not only for him but also for me, because I'd be going through the same thing next year.

I was also worried about going away with Brad. In a way I wanted to, but we hadn't been together for long and we were still at the snogging stage. I wasn't sure when, or if, I'd be ready to go beyond that. I really cared about him – he seemed to be perfect – but the trouble was I just didn't believe some of the things he said to me. I kept on thinking that I didn't deserve him and that, if we did sleep together, it would just be delaying the inevitable.

But there was a whole gang of us going together, so maybe it wouldn't come to that.

The phone rang while I was searching the job ads in the paper in the hope that somebody out there was looking for me. I picked it up anxiously, because it was the day of Brad's Maths A level and I was worried the paper had been so bad that he'd just walked out.

"Is that Jo Gibson?" a female voice said.

I said that it was, wondering who she was.

"This is Amy from Halo Productions. The roadshow, you know? We got your picture and we'd really like to see you. I was wondering if you could come in tomorrow at nine a.m.? We're using the hall at the sports centre for the auditions, it's just a formality, really. If it works out we're paying one hundred and fifty pounds for the day and you get a makeover and a haircut. And, of course, you'll be on TV. . ."

My stomach dived like I was on a roller coaster. I was so shocked that I dropped the phone. I just gaped at it for a moment as she gabbled on, then I picked it up again.

"So I'll see you tomorrow," she said.

I gulped. "I don't know. . ."

"You *will* come, Jo, won't you?" she said, chatting away as if I was her best friend.

"I . . . I didn't send you my picture," I said.

"What?"

I remembered the look on Brad's face when he'd told me I should send my picture in. "I think it was my boyfriend," I said, gritting my teeth and wondering if I had the strength to strangle him.

"Oh," she said. There was a pause as if she didn't know what to say. "We'd really like to see you anyway," she said eventually. "Your picture's great and you're the right height and everything. So will you come? It'll be a lot of fun."

"I'll try," I said; I didn't have the guts to say "no".

"Great!" she said. "See you tomorrow, Jo."

I put the phone down, thinking that I'd murder Brad. Then I went and studied myself in the mirror. My hair's long and straight and there's not much you can say about it. It's kind of normal, the colour's not too bad, it's light brown and it gets fair streaks in the summer. My face is OK, except I'd like my eyes to be bigger and my lips to be fuller. The problem is my body. On a good day, my breasts look like hillocks in the Sahara desert; they don't even fill a B-cup bra, although once I cheated and bought one anyway. (When I got home I padded it with tissues, but it didn't look right, so I've kept it in the hope I'll grow.) My waist isn't too bad, I guess — I can fit into a size ten, just about. The problem is my hips and thighs. They're gi-normous — absolutely huge! At least, they look that way compared to my breasts. There's a roll of fat around my middle too; all these years of Gran's food has turned into a swodge of flab and cellulite.

"I'll kill you, Brad!" I wailed. Then I jogged on the spot for ages in a vain bid to run the lard off.

I had no intention of actually going to the audition. I just wouldn't appear, and I'd leave the phone off the hook in case the pushy Amy called again.

I was annoyed with Brad; he'd had no right to do something like that.

* * *

He turned up a while later, looking pleased with himself.

"How dare you?" I began. I'd completely forgotten about his exam.

He frowned. "What?"

"The roadshow! You sent my picture off!"

"Oh, that." He grinned. "I was getting fed up with you always putting yourself down."

"They want me to go to an audition tomorrow," I moaned.

"They would, wouldn't they? I knew it, Jo. You look a lot better than you think you do."

His grin broadened. There was always something about Brad's smile that went straight to my heart. I could feel my anger melting, but I wasn't going to give up just yet.

"You should've asked me," I said.

"You'd've said no. Am I right?"

"No. I mean, yes, you're right. But I'd've liked to have had the choice."

Brad shrugged. "I thought you'd be pleased. You don't have to turn up." He held out his hand for mine. "Peace?"

I glared at him for a moment, then I gave him my hand. "Peace."

He hugged me. "Come on," he said. "Let's go and celebrate."

I remembered then about his exam. "How did it go?"

His eyes rolled. "I don't know. OK, I think. There

was one question that I made a mess of, but the others were OK. I might've got a B. That's all I need. But that's not why we're celebrating."

I looked at him. He pulled a letter out of his jacket pocket. It was from British Airways, asking him to go for a preliminary assessment for pilot training. It didn't say anything about grades, beyond that entrance to their training scheme depended upon candidates reaching an "acceptable" academic standard.

I jumped up and kissed his cheek. "That's great, Brad!"

He laughed. "I'm not there yet, but it's a start."

We went to the Cyber Café. At least it's supposed to be a Cyber Café, but because it's run by the local library, it's really cheap. We surfed the Net for a while, but Brad seemed distracted. I asked him what the matter was.

"It's the exams," he said, "I think I've done OK, but I keep on wondering if I've dropped a mark or two. There's so much riding on the results! I'll never get over it if I get Cs instead of Bs."

I thought about what he'd said. There wasn't much I could say because all he could do was to wait until August when the results came out. I shuddered – the whole process seems to be so mindlessly cruel. It's not the exams but the waiting; there must be some way they could get the grades out quicker, and let poor suffering souls like Brad out of their misery.

"You know what they say," I said. "If you want something enough, you'll find a way of getting it."

He winced. "That's not true, Jo, and you know it."

I sat back. There was a flying club just outside town. Brad had had a couple of lessons there, but he couldn't afford any more. If I got a job, and we didn't go on holiday. . .

"We'll save up and get you some more flying lessons," I said.

He rubbed his neck. "It'd take for ever." The company that his father worked for had gone bankrupt and he was out of work; his mother was a supply teacher and money was so tight that Brad would have to help out with some of his pay from his holiday job.

I could have kicked myself because I'd said the wrong thing. "We don't have to go to Spain," I said quickly.

He grinned. "Come on, Jo! The ferry's a tenner and the campsite is about a pound a day. It won't cost any more than fifty pounds each. And it'll be fun."

Suddenly, I thought of the one hundred and fifty pounds I'd get if I passed the audition for the TV roadshow. I smiled, but I didn't say anything, because I didn't want to get his hopes up.

"Come on," I said. "Let's try nasa.shuttle.com again. Maybe it's working now."

We linked up to the shuttle camera. As he watched the astronauts on their space walk, Brad's face lit up like a child's.

* * *

The next morning I spent a lot of time gazing in the mirror, telling myself what a fool I was. I didn't know what picture Brad had sent to the roadshow people, but I presumed that it must have been one taken of me from the waist up, because below that I was a mess.

If somebody had made one of those playing cards of me – you know, those shots that are split into the head, torso, legs and feet – nobody would ever suspect that my hips go with the rest of me.

My courage failed me for a moment, then I thought of the money and the way that Amy had said the audition was just a formality, so I put on a dress that has a flared skirt that hides my hips, and set off for the sports hall. I wasn't thinking of myself at all – I was thinking of Brad, more precisely the look I'd see on his face when I handed him a token for two flying lessons.

Although I'd felt like killing him at first, I know he did it to make me feel good about myself. The poor guy can't help it if he's blinded by love. (At least, I hope it's love.)

After all, I'd read in a magazine that the average British woman is a size sixteen, so by those standards, I wasn't too bad.

When I got to the hall, I nearly left, because there was a long line of girls waiting, and every one of them had a perfect figure. I recognized a few from school, but most of them were already working, and they looked unbelievably slim and incredibly beautiful. I just knew I had no right to be there, but as I turned to go I was accosted by a minute woman with a clipboard, who demanded my name.

I answered automatically and her face broke into a wide smile.

"Jo!" she said, "I'm Amy. I'm so glad you could make it. And you didn't lie about your height." She leaned towards me. "So many of them do, you know. It's absolutely hopeless. If you're under about five-five the camera makes you look like a gnome, you know?"

I didn't, but I nodded anyway.

Briskly, Amy told me what was going to happen. We all had to change into clothes they provided and walk down a cat-walk. There were professional models to show us how. So long as we didn't fall flat on our faces, we'd then get a haircut and make-up, and the show itself would be shot during the afternoon.

I asked her when I'd get the money.

Amy frowned and told me that if I passed the audition, they'd put a cheque in the post.

Then I was inside the hall, where they'd put up curtains to make an open-plan changing area. It was chaotic, full of girls waiting in line for the clothes they were supposed to put on and others milling around in bras and pants.

I felt terribly self-conscious, but I told myself it wasn't about me, it was about getting Brad his flying lessons.

The line moved slowly; the girl in front of me was wondering about her chances. "They only need twenty," she said, "and there's hundreds here." Her companion shrugged. "Who cares? It's just a laugh."

I was studying their rear ends. Both of them were just skin and bone; I wondered what it took to be so impossibly slim.

Then I reached the front of the queue.

"Size?" a girl asked.

I blanched, because I was supposed to wear tight hipster jeans with a lycra tank top.

"Twelve," I muttered, thinking of my flourishing hips. It's so unfair. If only the weight there would migrate to my breasts.

She looked me up and down. "Here's a ten," she said.

I took the jeans and went to change. They looked impossibly small. Suddenly, it didn't seem like such a good idea. If the girls in the queue were right, I didn't have much chance of being chosen.

And none at all if I couldn't get into the jeans.

Amy breezed past, smiling. "OK, Jo? Once you've changed, just go over there and they'll show you what to do."

I mumbled something, but she stayed around, so I took my shoes off and then I tried on the jeans under my dress. I was amazed when they got over my hips! I had to breathe in to do up the zip, but it wasn't as if I had to lie on the floor and struggle for hours.

When I had the top on, I looked in the mirror. It wasn't too bad.

As I stood in line waiting to be instructed in the fine art of walking, I felt a little like a bullock on the way to the slaughterhouse. I decided then and there that modelling wasn't my thing, and that once I'd got Brad his flying lessons, I'd never even pose for a photograph again.

The models were as cool as ice. Although they were wearing leggings and T-shirts, they looked incredibly poised and sure of themselves. I suppose they were revelling in being professionals, while the rest of us were just snivelling amateurs. Every so often, one of them would stalk down the hall to show us what to do; it wasn't so different from normal walking, but it was more of a stride – they kept their backs very straight and swung their arms.

Then we had to try as they watched. I wasn't looking forward to my turn. I could feel the tightness of the jeans and I was worried that they'd split.

One of the models came up to me, looking me up and down as she asked me my name.

As I told her, her eyes moved to my waist. "You know," she said, "you'd have a really nice figure if you lost some weight."

I breathed in, but she shook her head as she pinched the little roll of flab at my waist. "On camera, that'll look like a Michelin."

I cringed, but she didn't even notice. She went on down the line, in search of her next victim.

Then I realized that even if I *was* chosen, I didn't want to be seen on TV looking like the Michelin man!

I wouldn't be chosen anyway, because I was *fat*.

I turned away, and in the confusion of the crowd I managed to make it back to my own clothes. I changed quickly and left.

Amy didn't notice; if she had, I would have asked her if she got a kick out of humiliating people.

My face was flushed with embarrassment. I felt such a fool, so stupid for even going there!

As I walked away, the thought struck me that Brad might have sent me to the audition deliberately, knowing that someone was bound to tell me that I needed to lose weight. The idea was so awful that it actually hurt physically. But Brad's not devious; although we hadn't been going out for long I knew he'd never do anything like that.

Even so, it would be so awful if I lost him because of my podge!

I wandered around town for a bit, looking at the clothes on the mannequins in shop windows and knowing that I could never wear any of them.

Then I went home and cried for myself and for Brad's lost flying lessons. I couldn't help thinking how happy he'd have been if I'd been able to give them to him, and how he really deserved to have them. Things were tough enough for him without a girlfriend who was fat.

I persuaded myself that I would have got Brad

his flying lessons if I hadn't been so fat. It wasn't as if I was obese – I just had to lose some weight.

I decided then and there that I would go on a diet and get rid of my flab.

Chapter 2

That first week, I ate nothing but vegetables and fruit. I had to fight Gran; in the end, I told her I'd decided to turn vegetarian, so she gave up, muttering all the time about how young bodies need protein. My mother actually supported me; the company she works for had recently started a healthy living regime.

I'd weighed myself at the beginning of the week, but when I got on the scales seven days later, I hadn't lost so much as an ounce. I frowned, thinking that the scales had to be wrong; I was eating very little so I ought to be thin.

I stared at the pointer, but my weight stayed stubbornly the same. I'd been keeping away from the mirror, but when I looked at it I saw that the fat was still there.

I'd planned a treat for Brad to celebrate the end of his exams; I'd bought tickets for a new film that he wanted to see. It wasn't much, but it made me feel a bit better after the flying lessons fiasco. Brad's old fashioned; when we went out, he liked to pay for me, or at least for us to split the costs, even though I had more money than him because my parents gave me an allowance.

On the day of the last exam, I washed my hair and brushed it dry to get rid of the kinks at the end, then I spent ages deciding what to wear. In the end, I decided on jeans with sandals and a loose-ish top. I thought it looked OK, so long as I remembered to hold my stomach in.

I'd spent so long getting ready that I had to run to meet Brad; when I arrived I was panting, and my feet hurt from the sandals.

Brad was smiling, his face free of the worry that had been clouding it for so long.

"Hey!" he said. "You're looking good."

When I told him about the tickets, he grinned and kissed me on the cheek.

The film didn't interest me much – it was one of those action epics with lots of special effects – but Brad enjoyed it and as he watched with his arm around me I snuggled into him, happy just to be there.

When it ended and we walked out of the cinema, the world outside seemed quiet and pale, as it always does compared to Technicolor.

Brad was still smiling. "Let's go to PJ's," he said. "My treat."

PJ's is one of these American-style diners. It's *the* place to go but it's also expensive, so I began to protest, saying that I wasn't hungry.

"I am," Brad said. He wouldn't listen to my arguments — he virtually dragged me there.

When the waitress came to take our order, I asked for a salad, which is the cheapest thing on the menu, but Brad ignored me and asked for double bacon burgers for both of us, with cheese and fries and shakes and potato skins and sour cream on the side.

I winced, because a double bacon burger with cheese is my idea of heaven — at least, it had been before the roadshow. I'd spent the last week telling myself that it wasn't healthy to eat things like that.

"Brad. . ." I said, when the waitress had gone.

He leaned over and touched my lips with his forefinger. "I told you, it's my treat. It's only fair because you got the cinema tickets."

"But you. . ." I stopped, because Brad hated to be reminded of how little money he had.

He pulled out a twenty pound note from his pocket. "Dad told me to have a good time."

My eyes widened.

He leaned closer. "He's got a job, Jo. Deputy chief surveyor with the council."

Brad's eyes were shining. I was thrilled for him, because I knew how much it had hurt him, hurt the whole family, when the company had folded and his father had lost his job. Brad had told me that sometimes his father had sat up all night worrying and, during the time he'd been out of work, his hair had turned completely grey.

"That's great, Brad," I said.

"I know, Jo. I mean, there's not much chance of the council going bust."

I giggled. "I don't know about that. Dad's always suing them."

"You'll just have to tell him to go easy on them for a change!"

We just stared at each other for a while, then he sat back. "I didn't tell you, but I was thinking of giving up the idea of flying. I thought that if I could get a job, anything, it would make things easier at home."

"Oh Brad!" I blinked and thought, he's so good, I don't deserve him!

"But I don't have to now. The best part is that I can keep my wages so I'll be able to get a flying lesson or two. And we can definitely go to Spain."

The food came then: two vast oval plates that were filled to overflowing along with a huge bowl of potato skins. The burgers were at least ten centimetres high, almost too thick to pick up in your hands. Brad began to eat. I stared at my plate, thinking of the calories, thinking of the fat.

I didn't want any of it. At least, I told myself I didn't, but as I looked at it all my stomach yawned.

Brad frowned. "Is there anything wrong?"

"No," I said as I began to eat, "it's just that I've been on a diet this week."

His face flinched. "That's crazy, Jo. You don't need to lose weight."

"I do, Brad. You don't see it because I wear

loose clothes, but my hips and thighs are really fat."

He shook his head. I speared a french fry with my fork, but hesitated before I ate it.

"Look," Brad said, "eat the burger and the salad. Don't eat the cheese or the bun or the fries."

I felt really bad because he'd paid for it, but he ate my fries, so they weren't wasted.

"I suppose you don't want a double chocolate ice-cream with hot fudge sauce and brownies?" he said, when we'd finished.

"You're right!" I said.

He ordered one and ate the lot, but he's six feet tall so he's got plenty of room for it.

We walked home hand in hand.

"You know," he said, "I wish you wouldn't go on a diet."

"Why not?"

"You don't need to, really you don't."

"I *do*, Brad! I *am* fat! You just don't see it."

He winked. "Maybe I will one of these days."

"Brad!"

"Seriously, Jo." He let go of my hand and put his arm around me, pulling me close. "If you needed to go on a diet I'd tell you, but honestly, you don't."

"Don't lie to me, Brad."

"I'm not lying. I'm just worried. . ."

I looked at him. "Worried about what?"

Brad's expression had become wistful. "You hear these stories about girls going on diets, and the next thing, they're starving themselves to death. They end up in hospital looking like famine victims."

"Don't be ridiculous!" I snapped. "That would never happen to me."

"Why take the chance, Jo? Why not give up the diet and go jogging instead?"

I didn't say anything, I was thinking. When we reached my house, I didn't ask him in; my parents were there and it would have been a big scene – you know, my mother would have made coffee and my father would have sat him down for a man-to-man chat. My parents knew I was seeing him, but they kept on saying things like I'm too young to be serious about anyone. They treated my feelings as a joke, and it hurt when they dismissed Brad as a childish crush.

"See you tomorrow?" he said.

I nodded.

"If it's a nice day," he said, "we could get the train to the coast."

I smiled, but inside I was praying for rain. I couldn't bear the thought of Brad seeing me in a swimsuit, or even shorts.

For once, my prayers were answered. We went to Brad's the next day. His parents were out and we sat on the sofa watching a video, then we started kissing. And then things got a little heavy. Brad must have sensed I wasn't happy because he broke off and asked me if I was OK.

"It's no big deal," he said. Then he smiled as he brushed my hair back. "I mean, it *is* a big deal, but if you don't want to, I'll have to live with it."

I stood up. "It's not that. I'm just. . ."

"Just what?"

"I'm just not ready." I didn't say the rest of it — that I was scared of making a fool of myself, scared, too, that he wouldn't want me afterwards. We'd never actually talked about it, but I was pretty sure that Brad had slept with the girl he'd been going out with before me.

"I mean," I went on, "we haven't been together very long."

I was so embarrassed that I felt my face burn. Brad went and got some Coke from the fridge.

"Look," he said, "you don't need to make excuses. Everybody has to lose their virginity sometime, you know."

My face was absolutely blazing as I sipped my Coke. It wasn't Diet, but it was something to do. I avoided looking at him and thought instead about all that sugar turning into fat. He came over and put his arms around me, then he kissed my neck. I shuddered, then I loosened his grip on me and turned to face him.

"It just doesn't feel right yet, Brad."

"OK, Jo. But will you tell me when it does?"

"Yes."

"I like you a lot, you know."

"I like you too."

It was different after that. I left and went home,

because there was a distance between us. I was afraid that Brad would change his mind about me because I'd turned him down. Then I wondered if I really did care for him as much as I thought; if I did, surely I'd want to go to bed with him?

And I felt really awful about drinking that Coke.

When Brad started work at the end of June, he was on late shifts, which meant I had the day to myself. I gave myself another week to get a real job before I went along to be the dogsbody in my father's law firm. I didn't jog, but I did go to the tennis club, where I played games with the girls from school.

And I stuck to my vegetarian diet, despite Gran's protests and hurt looks. Maddie was in Paris doing work experience, but she was due home soon. I thought it would be easier when she was at home, because she didn't like Gran's cooking either.

Then Naomi phoned one afternoon. I was surprised, because the last time we'd spoken, she'd been pretty bitter. And so was I. We'd been friends for years, and it wasn't as if she'd been going out with Brad or anything like that. It was just that she'd met him first, and because of that, she thought she had a right to him. The trouble was, Brad had paid no attention to her. Straight off, he'd started talking to me.

Naomi apologized for the things she'd said and in the end, we agreed to meet for a chat.

We went to a café in town. Naomi was looking good – she'd been on holiday and she had a great tan. She was wearing a black halter top and white jeans and when I saw her I wondered yet again why, of the two of us, Brad had chosen me. When I'm with Naomi, I always feel big and clumsy.

She asked me how I was doing, and I rambled on for a while before I told her about my diet and that Brad had said that I didn't need to lose weight. It was the first time I'd mentioned his name.

"Look, Jo," she said, "there's no hard feelings. If you want to talk about Brad, you can."

"It's not Brad so much as I feel terribly fat," I said mournfully. "I'm on a diet, but it's not working."

"Some men like women to be – you know, well padded," she said. "I think the word is Rubenesque. You know all these nudes by Old Masters? Most of them are pretty fat."

"Yeah, but I don't want to be like that. I'm nearly seventeen years old and I'd like to be able to wear hipsters and boob tubes and things like that without my stomach hanging out all over the place. I'd like to be able to go into a shop and buy what I want. I only ever buy things that hide my weight."

Naomi nodded as if she understood.

"Come on!" I said. "You don't even know what I'm talking about."

"I do," she said. "D'you remember when Sadie was really fat?"

Sadie's Naomi's cousin. She broke her leg and when she was in plaster the weight really piled on.

"I know what she went through," Naomi went on. "Thing is, it's all about body image, Jo. If you feel that you're fat, then you are. You've got to think yourself slim."

"It's not as easy as that."

"It's not so difficult either. Sadie went on this diet, one thousand calories a day. The first week she didn't lose anything, but after that it just slid off."

I didn't know much about calories, only about sugar and fat.

"You can buy diet stuff," Naomi said. "It's a couple of hundred calories. You have that instead of a meal."

I sighed as I wondered what Gran would say.

"I haven't told you my news," Naomi said. "I've got a job in Breeze."

I blinked. Breeze is a really cool clothes shop, selling designer gear at outrageous prices. I'd never even dared to go through the door.

"How did you manage that?"

"There was a sign in the window saying *Help Wanted*, so I went in and I got the job. I'm starting tomorrow. You've got to come and see me, Jo. You can try things on. It'll be fun."

I smiled.

"And that's not all," she said. "I met a boy on holiday."

I huddled closer. "Tell me more."

"He's nineteen, he's a student, but he's working at the camp site in Cornwall over the summer. Thing is, he's at the University of Surrey, so during term-time he's not so far away."

"Are you seeing him again?"

"He wants me to go down next month for the weekend. I said I would. I just have to work out a way to get my parents to go along with it." She leaned close. "I was wondering, could I say that I was going to stay with you?"

I laughed and we began to plot.

Afterwards, I bought a diet book, one that listed the calorie content of all foods at the back. I winced when I saw that butter had seven hundred and fifty calories per hundred grams, and cheese about three hundred and fifty. Gran smothered vegetables with butter and she often served a cheese sauce on the side.

No wonder I hadn't lost any weight! I thought.

I began to skip meals. I would tell Gran that I was having lunch out, then I wouldn't bother to eat anything. At first I felt really hungry, but after a couple of days my body got used to the lack of food. It worked to an extent, but not very well because every time I got back there would be a quiche or an omelette or even a pizza. By this time Gran had almost given in to my vegetarianism, but she was still determined to feed me good, wholesome stodge.

Pizza is a hopeless diet food; it has zillions of calories. The thing is, Gran takes it as a personal insult if you don't eat every scrap on your plate.

So it became a campaign of stealth. I'd wait until Gran's back was turned, then I would wrap most of the pizza or whatever it was in a paper napkin and throw it into the bin. As long as I didn't get rid of too much at once, she didn't notice what I was doing.

When I weighed myself again, I'd lost three pounds.

It wasn't much, but at least it was a start. I reckoned that I needed to lose about a stone and a half.

My weight loss wasn't so great that Brad noticed it, and we didn't eat out because he was saving up for his flying lessons. He wanted to go solo before he went to see BA, and that meant quite a few hours.

What Naomi had said troubled me, so one day I asked him once if he liked fat women.

He frowned. "What gave you that idea?"

"You're always nagging me when I say I'm on a diet."

"Jo! You don't need to diet. I don't want you to get obsessed with your weight. You're not fat. If you were I'd tell you, but you're not."

Like I said, Brad suffered from a peculiar visual impairment; he just did not see my flab.

Because he was working shifts, we were never alone together and I was glad about that. I began at Dad's office and it wasn't too bad, although the secretaries were a bit funny with me because I was the boss's daughter. At last I was out of Gran's clutches! Breakfast was a rush so she didn't notice that I wasn't eating much, and I didn't have to make excuses to avoid lunch. At work, most days I just had an apple, although sometimes I skipped food entirely.

There was only dinner. It was almost always at least eight hundred calories, sometimes more than a thousand, and I only ever managed to do away with about half of it.

I couldn't avoid it either, because if I said I was going out, Gran would make dinner early, and if I came back late, it would be waiting for me when I got home.

Although I love Gran, I began to dislike her; she was obviously determined to keep me fat.

I didn't know what to do about it; although I was losing weight, I was losing it so slowly that it would be months before I reached my target. I thought about getting a waitressing job in the evenings, but my parents weren't happy about me being out late every night and besides, it would have meant that I would never see Brad at all.

I began to despair, then all of a sudden I had a lucky break. Gran announced that she was going to see her sister in Canada, and I realized that when she was away, I could diet to my heart's content!

Chapter 3

I printed a big capital M on my computer and stuck it on the wall by my mirror to remind myself of the weight I had to lose. The M stands for motivation, the key to making a diet work. You have to be absolutely determined to get rid of the flab. My diet book told me that I had to be clear about my objectives too, so when Dad gave me my first pay, I went to the mall and bought myself a pair of size eight jeans and a clingy top that looked like a child's. Then I hung them on front of my wardrobe, where I'd see them all the time. I told myself that I had to get into them, else I'd've wasted the money that I'd spent.

I'd worked out that I needed to lose a stone and a half; if I did that, I'd be a size eight.

I was hovering around nine stones at that point, and I figured that a healthy weight for me would be about seven and a half stones. I planned to take about 1,000 calories a day, so I reckoned it would take me about two months to lose the weight. I started on an exercise programme too; I jogged for an hour in the evenings and I went to the gym four times a week. That way, I hoped I'd reached my target weight in six weeks or so.

Next to the big M, I pinned up a picture of Dory Lyon; she was a perfect size eight. I'd never make it as a model, but if I lost the flab I wouldn't look quite so bad.

With Gran away, Mum bought a load of ready-prepared meals and salad stuff. My parents get home from work late so they eat after me. Mum told me to help myself to meals, but I usually made a big bowl of salad and ate that with cottage cheese and fruit juice. I was really looking forward to weighing myself after the first week.

Brad phoned from the hospital on Friday night. "I'm missing you," he said.

"Mmm hmm," I murmured. I was missing him too, but in a way I was glad because I could concentrate on my diet.

"I've got Sunday off," he said. "I've got a flying lesson in the morning – d'you want to come with me? We could have a picnic down by the river if it's nice."

"OK," I said.

I spent all of Saturday deciding what to wear. I pulled everything out of my wardrobe, but nothing was right. The size eight jeans taunted me. I managed to get into the lycra top but I looked like a tramp. It was so tight that you could see every line of my bra and it made my breasts look like the salt flats of Utah.

Naomi called midway through this to ask me if I was doing anything that night, and I pretended that I was seeing Brad. I didn't feel up to seeing her because I looked such a mess.

Naomi's one of these people who always manage to look just right. As soon as a new fad starts, she's got it, just like that. A lot of the girls were jealous of her, but she'd been my best friend for ever and I'd become used to it.

It's not as if she was bitchy – she always offered to lend me clothes, but she's smaller than I am so they didn't fit.

I put the phone down and went back to my ruminations. If only I hadn't bought these size eight jeans and that silly top, I could have afforded something new! I sighed deeply and settled on my old standby – black jeans and a baggy T-shirt I'd bought in Arizona on holiday last year.

It wasn't Dolce & Gabbana, but at least it would do.

Brad picked me up early on Sunday morning. He was driving his mother's Fiesta; he only passed his test a few months ago but he drives really well. Now that his father's working again, he's ordered a 4WD and Brad was looking forward to driving that.

He was so excited about his flying lesson. He'd

put the money to pay for it in an envelope and as we drove to the airfield, he asked me to count it to make sure that it was all there.

When we got to the airfield, Brad went off with the instructor while I went into the office to watch. It was a beautiful morning. The sky was an unblemished blue, but the wind-sock was a rigid right angle against its tether and from listening to the other flyers I gathered that there was a strong headwind. I watched Brad and his instructor walk to the plane; there was a pause as they made the pre-flight checks and then the little Cessna rolled to the end of the runway and stood bracing itself to take off.

The plane's engine roared like an angry gnat and then it began to lumber down the runway, gathering speed until it lifted jerkily into the air at the other end.

I've always loved flying, although I've only ever flown in commercial jets, but my heart thudded and my stomach fluttered and I felt a little of the thrill that I knew Brad was experiencing right then. He's asked me to go up with him when the instructor says it's OK, but that won't be for a while yet.

I smiled as I watched the plane circle over the airfield and then it turned towards the hills beyond the town. The wings juddered slightly, and I gasped inwardly, because I'd sensed that Brad had taken over the controls. I fetched a bitter black coffee from the machine, and then I settled down to read a magazine.

After a while a woman in a flying jacket came in, untangling her long blonde hair that had been blown awry by the wind. She looked at me and grinned.

"Hi!" she said. "I'm Suzy. Are you my lesson?"

I gaped. "No, I'm just waiting for my boyfriend."

She frowned as she glanced at her watch, then she got a coffee too and sat down opposite me.

"We're doing a special offer," she said, "fifty pounds for the first two lessons. Are you interested? I think my client's chickened out."

My stomach turned over. "I've never thought about learning to fly," I said slowly. "I'm just sort of hanging around. My boyfriend wants to be an airline pilot."

She laughed. "Don't we all?"

A car pulled up outside then, and a woman got out.

"Ah, here she is now," she said, getting up. "If you change you mind, let me know. The offer's only good for a couple of weeks."

I stood up to watch as the two women headed for the plane. I thought about what the instructor had said but the idea of trying to fly myself gave me terrible jitters. Apart from anything else, I couldn't afford it, although my father would probably give me the money if I asked.

Brad's hour was nearly over. I watched the horizon until I saw a blip appear and then I gazed at the Cessna as it circled over the airfield and came into land, bouncing just once as the wheels hit the tarmac. It taxied back to the hangar and a few minutes later Brad appeared.

He was exhilarated; there was a sheen of sweat on his forehead and his body was taut with excitement, although as we drove away his mood changed.

"What is it?" I asked.

His hands tightened on the steering wheel. "I landed OK," he said, "but when we were up there I nearly stalled. I wasn't watching the artificial horizon properly, I was watching the real horizon instead. It's perspective, y'see. I nearly put us into a dive. The instructor had to take over the controls."

I didn't really understand what he was talking about. "Isn't that what instructors are for?"

"I should've known, Jo. I've never done it before but I've read about it."

"It's not the same thing," I said carefully.

"It's the kind of thing that would make me fail an aptitude test."

"If you know about it, you won't do it again."

"But it was such a stupid thing to do! I could've kicked myself. It's the kind of thing that idiots do the first time they're up there."

I looked at Brad. His profile was strong and determined. For the first time, I realized that, like me, he was a perfectionist.

"How many times have you flown, Brad?"

"That was my third hour, but it's only the second time I took the controls."

"Did the instructor say you don't have aptitude?"

He winced. "No," he said. "He said I was doing really well. He said everybody makes the same mistake. He did himself."

"Well, then."

His hand left the steering-wheel and rested briefly on my knee. He smiled. "Thanks, Jo," he said.

When we reached the car park at the riverside, Brad took a Sainsbury's bag and a rug from the boot, then we walked way along the path until we were far away from other people. The wind had gone, and the day was becoming very warm. He spread the rug over the grass, then we sat down together.

"I'm starving," he said, as he reached into the bag. There were cans of Coke, crisps, sandwiches, cheesecake and apples.

My stomach rumbled. I'd been on salads and cottage cheese all week and it felt like I hadn't eaten at all.

Brad gnawed at a cob loaded with ham salad and mayonnaise. "C'mon," he said.

I picked up an apple and began to eat, telling myself that it was only forty or so calories. I was still hungry as Brad started on a second cob. As I watched him eat, the rumble in my stomach became a roar.

I thought of the calories; there must have been about six hundred in each cob and Brad had had two, but because of his male physiology it didn't result in so much as an ounce of fat.

My stomach was yawning like the Grand Canyon. I couldn't help noticing that there was one cob left and once I'd noticed, I couldn't help staring at it.

I felt like a junkie in search of a fix. Unbidden, my hand strayed towards the food and I felt an illicit thrill as my fingers folded around the soft roll. I told myself I'd only take a bite or two but the first bite tasted heavenly, so I finished it, mayonnaise and all.

I felt so guilty that I blushed, but Brad didn't notice. He'd opened the bag of crisps and was devouring them.

I had one or two, not too many. Then Brad opened the cellophane box that held two slabs of cheesecake. I stared at it as if it was the forbidden fruit, wondering if I dared, but knowing that I shouldn't.

"If you don't want it, I'll have it," he said, as if a slice of lemon cheesecake was nothing at all.

Brad had no idea of my dilemma, no idea that that cheesecake would mean days, even weeks of lettuce and hunger pangs. I picked up the box and saw that the cake contained four hundred and sixty-three calories, most of them in the form of fat. My metabolism acts like a magnet for fat – every last gram goes straight to my hips.

"Go on," he said.

I took a bite, just one, and felt the soft squishy

cream on my tongue. It was gone too quickly, too deliciously, so I took another and then another one, hating myself all the time. I had all the self-control of a two-year-old.

Brad still hadn't touched his cheesecake. He was watching me with a quirky smile on his face.

"You want it, Jo?"

"I couldn't. . ." I was drooling like a Labrador.

Carefully, he divided the cake in two and handed me half.

"You shouldn't."

"I couldn't eat it all myself with you watching me like that."

I was too busy guzzling it to say thank you.

Afterwards, I imagined the cheesecake in my stomach, mixed with the crisps and the cob and the mayonnaise, the fat migrating through my veins, following signposts that led it straight to my thighs.

I told myself that I should feel sick, but I felt wonderful, all sort of dreamy and soft, and there beside me was the boy I adored.

Brad lay back and pulled me down.

"OK, honey?" he asked. "You've gone all quiet of a sudden." He pulled the tab of a can of Coke and I felt the spray on my face.

"I'm fine," I said, thinking that I would be if I hadn't eaten so much food. I counted up and stopped, horrified, when I realized that I'd eaten way over fifteen hundred calories and I still had the ritual of Sunday dinner with my parents to get through.

"Y'know," Brad went on, "when this year started

off it was really grim. Dad was unemployed, and when I wrote to the airlines they said they weren't recruiting trainee pilots this year. They told me to try the RAF."

He winced, because although he lived for flying, he was also devoutly pacifist; his principles would never allow him to learn to fly for the purpose of killing people. It was one of the things that I respected about him.

"Dad got depressed when he didn't get another job quickly, and I was pretty down too, because I was sure I wasn't going to get a job flying. The worst thing was, Dad was so good about it. He told me to keep trying. He was the one who discovered that BA were doing a training scheme after all. But it was heartbreaking watching him. He used to get up in the morning and because he had nothing to do all day he used to do things around the house, like he stripped the loft and re-insulated it, then he built an extra bedroom. Mum started to bitch at him because of the mess. But it wasn't the mess, it was the stress. The tension got to us all. I was below zero when I met you. I thought, what can a girl like this see in me? What can anybody see in me? I was that low."

He smiled as his arm tightened around me. "When we got together, things began to get better," he said.

"I didn't do anything," I said quickly.

"Yes, you did, Jo. You listened. When I told you I wanted to be a pilot, you didn't laugh; you started to help me figure out a way of doing it. When you found out I didn't have much money, you never ever said you wanted to do anything that cost money. But if there was a film on that I wanted to see, you always managed to get some tickets somehow."

"That's nothing," I said. My parents aren't millionaires, but they're quite well off and they've always been fairly generous with Maddie and me.

"It's not nothing, it's an awful lot," he replied. "At least, it means a lot to me. It means that you like me for what I am, not what I have or what I do. A lot of girls aren't like that, you know. If you don't have any money, they don't want to know."

"They'll want to know when you're a pilot," I said.

"Ah, yes, but you want to know me now. That's what counts, Jo."

He leaned closer, his face blotted out the sun and then he kissed me and my heart began to beat like a drum. For a moment, I forgot all about the calories and my hips and my thighs, and all I cared about was being with Brad. I could feel myself falling in love with him, tumbling down into a cocoon of warmth and happiness where nothing mattered except being with him.

Brad rolled on top of me, his arms folded around my shoulders, and then one hand strayed down my T-shirt, towards my left breast. Just as I began to think of my measly pimples, a dog barked and he pulled away.

For a moment he gazed deep into my eyes, and then he kissed my forehead.

"I'm crazy about you, Jo. I really am."

A thrill ran through me and I shivered.

The dog came closer and with it the sounds of people. Our reverie was disturbed. Brad smiled as they passed, then he turned back to me and ran his hands down my side. I jumped because I didn't want him to reach my fat hips, and as I jerked up the button of my jeans popped off.

I gasped as my face burned with embarrassment.

Brad laughed. "Serves you right for eating so much cheesecake!" he teased.

I didn't even smile. My stomach lurched and I felt sick inside. All the fat and carbohydrates in my digestive system rumbled and threatened to come back on me.

I stood up.

Brad frowned. "What's wrong?"

"Nothing," I said, as I began to pack wrappings back in the bag. The day had changed somehow; now it felt cold despite the sun.

Brad stood up, shaking his head. "Have I done something to upset you?"

"No. I've just remembered, we've got people coming. Mum asked me to get back early."

It was a lie, the first I had ever told him.

In the car on the way home, I didn't say a word.

At dinner, I didn't eat much, I just toyed with my vegetables.

My mother asked if I was all right, so I told her that I'd eaten a big lunch with Brad.

"You'll have to bring him home for a meal sometime," she said.

I winced. She'd said "hello" to Brad one time when he'd walked me home, but Dad hadn't even met him yet. The Gibsons *en famille* can be a daunting experience, one that I didn't want to subject him to yet.

After dinner, I went upstairs and spent a long time gazing at the bathroom scales. I'd been looking forward to this moment all week, but now that it had come, I was afraid.

Very slowly, I put one foot on to the scales and watched the needle quiver. I hovered for an age, and then I stepped on with both feet. The needle wavered wildly between ten and eight stones. It took a long time to settle at eight stones thirteen pounds.

I gaped and then I got off the scales and waited for a while before I weighed myself again.

Eight stones and thirteen pounds!

For a whole week I'd eaten nothing but salad and cottage cheese, no dressing. I had been constantly hungry, my mind tormented by thoughts of food, but I'd only lost a measly pound, if that. At this rate, it would take me *five months* to get to my target weight!

And Brad had teased me about the button popping on my jeans.

I went to my bedroom, where I threw myself down on my bed and cried.

Chapter 4

When I woke up the next morning, I felt delicious and soft, remembering the day before and all the nice things that Brad had said. I was really happy for a moment, because nobody had ever said anything like that to me before, especially not a boy that I cared about.

And then I remembered what had happened afterwards, when the button on my jeans had popped. Brad must have seen then how plump I am.

My stomach clenched into a hard, angry ball.

If I didn't lose weight, I might lose him – boys just don't like girls who are fat. After a moment "might" became "would". I lay there thinking that I couldn't cope if I lost the boy that I was beginning to love.

Thoughts drifted through my mind, mostly of the food I had eaten yesterday. The cob and the crisps and the cheesecake haunted me – floating in my head like these illustrations on menus from the Little Chef — fatty, sugary, *killing* food made to look delicious just so that some business man can make a profit out of it.

I hated myself for my weakness, my lack of self control. So much for my M for Motivation! In just a moment I had forgotten, gorged myself like a milking cow.

What to do now?

I got up and, steeling myself, took off the T-shirt I slept in so that I could study my body in the mirror. I looked disgusting — unbelievably gross! My dime-size breasts were like those of a child, whilst my thighs were tree trunks, solid fat dimpled with cellulite. And as for my waist and hips — there was a roll of fat around my torso and another below my waist. I grabbed it with both hands, and both hands were full.

I closed my eyes and thought, *If only I could get rid of it!* If I wasn't so fat, my breasts wouldn't look so small. If I was slim and lithe, I could wear the clothes that I wanted to wear, and Brad would love me for ever.

The size eight jeans hung on my wardrobe; I took them off the hanger, sat down on my bed and tried to wriggle in, but I couldn't even get them over my thighs. They seemed so impossibly tiny that I would never get into them. Dory Lyon gazed at me disdainfully from the picture I'd clipped out. I looked at her and thought, if she can do it, so can I.

But how? I'd only been on a proper calorie controlled diet for a week, and after just six days I'd ruined it. I put my T-shirt on again and sat down to think.

I began to waver. I told myself it was only a thousand extra calories I'd taken; if I cut my diet to seven hundred and fifty calories a day, I'd lose the effects in just four days. It would be horrible, but I'd been so weak, I deserved to suffer.

On the other hand, if I ate nothing at all today, then I'd make it up in just twenty-four hours. But that was fasting, and I'd read somewhere that fasting isn't good for you.

Then I remembered an article I'd read about supermodels. One of them said that every so often she goes on a detoxifying fast. During the first day, she takes nothing but herbal tea, and on the second and third only fruit and raw vegetables. In the picture that went along with the article, the supermodel looked healthy enough.

I thought about it, wondered if I had the self control to eat nothing and drink only herbal tea for twenty-fours hours, and then decided I *had* to do it. If I wanted to keep Brad, I had no choice.

If only I could get through today, tomorrow I could go back to salads and cottage cheese. One day without food is nothing; millions of people in the world go hungry every day.

That was the moment I began to go mad.

That first day was funny. On the way to Dad's

office, I stopped at the healthfood shop and bought a packet of camomile tea-bags. The label said camomile tea had no calories at all and it was also supposed to have a calming effect.

Dad's got a case that's been going on for ever. It involves a motorway extension that the government's planning, and he's acting for all the people whose houses will end up next to it. They're pretty cheesed off because when the houses were built fifteen years ago the outlook was your archetypical rural bliss.

According to Dad and the owners, the government's compensation offer isn't enough. I spent the whole morning searching the files for the original planning applications and consents and so forth. Nobody said anything when I worked through my lunch hour.

My stomach was gnawing, but I ignored it and after a while it went away.

I felt truly virtuous that night when I went to bed. Not so much as a single calorie had passed my lips.

The next day, I didn't eat breakfast as usual and then when lunchtime came I realized that I could do without food, so I did. For dinner, I had some steamed asparagus, no butter, and two apples for dessert.

As I went to bed that night, I felt giddy and light-headed; it was all the fat that was working its way out of my system, I thought.

* * *

Naomi and I met up at the juice bar in the mall. I groaned when I saw her, because she looked like a star. She'd had her hair cut and tinted. It used to be mousey brown, but now it's just the right side of blonde, and she was wearing a spandex top with cycling shorts and DKNY trainers. There just wasn't so much as an ounce of fat anywhere. According to the magazines, it's *the* look of the summer, but they're giving all these warnings about not everybody being able to carry it off.

She smiled gleefully and told me she got it all at twenty-five per cent discount because she works in Breeze. She ordered mango and peach juice; I had carrot, which tasted suspiciously sweet, although it was supposed to be pure. I took a sip and then left it.

"Remember what I said last time?" she began, with a wheedling look on her face.

I didn't, but I nodded anyway.

"Well, Mark rang last night, and he wants me to go down to Cornwall this weekend. Will you, like, will you cover for me? I mean, if I tell them I'm with you. . ."

I frowned. When we'd talked before, I didn't think she'd actually go through with it. Planning to go away for a dirty weekend and actually doing it are two different things. "What if they ring? If Mum or Dad answer, that'll be it."

Naomi shook her head vigorously. "They won't. They trust you. And I'll ring them just to make sure. Come on, Jo, it's really important to me. They'd never let me go if they knew I was going to stay with Mark. It's not as if you have to do anything, it's just that if you bump into Mum or something, she might mention it."

I didn't want to do it. I'm not sure why not, but something told me we'd get found out.

"Please, Jo," Naomi pleaded. "Mark's the first boy I've met in ages. I really like him a lot and it would be awful if it all got screwed up just because I can't go to see him and he meets someone else."

My grandmother's voice rang out in my head: *If he really likes you, he'll wait for you.* She's always saying things like that; in her way of things, boys only want One Thing and any girl who even thinks about it is Just A Tart.

"It's all right for you, you've got Brad," Naomi said.

"OK," I said slowly. There was no reason to, I know, but I did feel guilty because she'd been hurt.

She grinned. "How's things? Are you seeing him this weekend?"

I toyed with the celery stick that came with my carrot juice. "He's working. He likes doing weekends, because he gets extra money. But we're going to that new movie on Friday night."

I'd been eating only vegetables and a little fruit all week, four hundred calories a day, if that. I was looking forward to surprising Brad with my new slim figure, but I didn't want him going on about my diet again. I changed the subject.

"Are you going to sleep with Mark?"

Naomi blushed, then she smiled. "What makes you think I haven't slept with him already?"

I gazed at her. "Naomi! You lost your virginity and you didn't tell me?"

Her smiled broadened. "We fell out, remember? And there wasn't much of my virginity left after that party at Greg's."

I blushed at the memory. Greg's parents had been away, and there'd been this punch which was virtually one hundred per cent pure vodka. Naomi had ended up in bed with Siggy Thomas, who she'd then fancied like crazy, and it had been pretty heavy, although they hadn't actually gone all the way.

"What was it like?"

"You mean you and Brad. . .?"

I shook my head.

Naomi sat back and flexed her arms against the seat. I could tell that she was working out what to say to me. "It was . . . well, it was OK. It wasn't great, but then it's not supposed to be, the first time. At least, they say it often isn't. But it was sort of nice. I was so nervous, I was shaking all over. And we were in Mark's tent. It wasn't exactly the world's most romantic spot."

She was still smiling, but there was a poignant look in her eyes. I suddenly felt terribly sorry for her. She'd been thinking about losing her virginity for ages – we'd both been thinking about it, but we'd never thought then that the whole thing might turn out to be an anti-climax. We'd been more worried that we'd gain some sort of aura, a signal that told everybody, in particular our parents, that our maidenheads were gone.

My father's not what you'd call liberated, but my mother's quite mature about sex. It's not a prohibited subject or anything like that, but she also says it's a big step and it's very important to be sure of your feelings and things like that. She's never actually said so, but I know that she thinks that sixteen is a bit too young, and she's absolutely paranoid about AIDS and pregnancy. Naomi's parents are a lot more strict. They'd have a fit if they found out about her and Mark.

"At least it's over," Naomi said brightly.

I didn't know what to say to her. We left the juice bar and meandered through the mall. On the way home, we passed Breeze. There was a dreamy dress in the window; it was silver grey and it shimmered in the lights like spangled gauze.

Naomi's eyes danced as we looked at it. "I tried it on the other day," she said. "There are a couple in the back of the shop. The manageress told me that I could borrow one for the weekend, so long as I bring it back in one piece. In the disco at Newquay, it'll knock them dead!"

I giggled. We linked arms as we walked the rest of the way home. It felt good to be friends again.

"You won't forget?" Naomi asked me when we reached her house.

"Course not. Just so long as you don't blame me if they find out anyway."

"They won't," she said.

* * *

The movie had a misleading title. We'd thought it was a thriller but it turned out to be a weepy, because the good guy's wife was dying of cancer. Midway through, I could tell that Brad was getting bored, but I was loving it. He draped his arm around me tolerantly as I sobbed my way through it.

Afterwards, as we walked home, he said: "I hope all this overtime I'm doing won't affect us. I'm doing fours hours extra today and tomorrow, but it means that I'll get about one hundred pounds for the weekend alone."

"That's good," I replied.

"You don't mind?"

"Nope."

"Hey!" He stopped walking and faced me. "Don't you want to see me, Jo?"

I smiled to myself. The waistband of the skirt I was wearing wasn't nearly as tight as it had been two weeks ago, and I couldn't wait for him to see me in those size eight jeans!

"Of course I do. I just understand you need the money," I said.

He gazed at me. "I don't want to lose you, Jo."

"You won't." I stood up on tiptoe and planted a kiss on his cheek. I was pleased, because I'd been afraid that *I* would lose *him*.

We began to walk again and he put his arm around my waist and hugged me tight. Then he frowned. "You've lost weight," he said.

I was thrilled. "Mmm hmm."

"You're not still going on that crazy diet, are you?"

"Why not? On Sunday you were teasing me about my jeans."

"I didn't, Jo."

"You did! You said it was my fault for eating too much cheesecake!"

He laughed. "I didn't mean it like that. It was just a joke. You don't need to diet, Jo. You really don't."

"I'm not going to much longer," I said. "I just need to lose another pound or two. I want to look good on the beach when we go to Spain."

Brad's expression was very serious. "I don't want you to diet, Jo."

I began to shake my head. Although he was my boyfriend, it wasn't really his business whether I dieted or not.

"You really don't. There's a girl I know. She wasn't fat but she went on a diet anyway. She ended up looking like an Auschwitz survivor. She was in hospital for months and months and she's still really ill."

I stopped dead. "Do I *look* like an Auschwitz survivor, Brad?"

"No, but I don't want you to take the risk. You can be really obsessive about things, Jo. Everything has to be perfect. Those models in magazines, they don't look so good in real life. You're just fine the way you are."

"Bursting jeans and all? Like I'm an ageing, overweight housewife who doesn't exercise enough? Gee, thanks!"

"I didn't mean it like that, Jo. Please don't diet. You don't need to."

"What's it to you, anyway?"

He sighed deeply. "I care about you, Jo. I really do. Right now, I don't have much money or time, but if I get on to the pilot training scheme, things will be different for us. I'll be able to get discount air tickets and we can fly all over the world together."

Some chance! I thought to myself. If Brad did get on to the pilot training scheme, he'd probably fall for a flight attendant with a figure like Kate Moss.

"You call me obsessive," I argued, "but you're the one who's getting strung up about it."

He sighed again. "OK," he said, "I'll tell you the truth. The girl I know . . . it's my sister."

I gaped at him. I didn't know he had a sister. As far as I knew, the family was only Brad and his little brother, Aidan. He'd never mentioned a sister before.

"She's twenty-four now," he said. "Her name's Lucy. Nobody around here knows her because when we moved here, she'd just started at Uni and she wasn't at home. That's when she got ill. She just stopped eating and she ended up in intensive care. She only weighed five stones. Ever since then, she's been in and out of hospital. It's anorexia. Her life's miserable, Jo, it really is. I mean, she's intelligent, she's got a great personality, she could have a wonderful life, but all she cares about is being thin."

Brad's face was drawn; I could see that whatever had happened to Lucy had hurt him a lot. Maybe that was why he hadn't mentioned her.

"I'd hate it if that happened to you, Jo."

I smiled. "It won't, Brad. About a third of the women in this country are on a diet at any one time. Not everyone gets anorexia, you know."

"I know that. I just don't want you to take the risk, that's all."

I hugged him. "I won't."

"Promise?"

"Promise."

The weekend passed. My thoughts flitted between Brad at work, and Naomi with Mark. I had a horrible feeling that that relationship wasn't going to work out and I felt terribly sorry for her.

A couple of years ago, we'd both pledged that we wouldn't sleep with a boy until we were sure of him, and she wasn't sure of Mark because she thought she'd lose him if she didn't go down for the weekend the first time he asked.

Was I sure of Brad? Well, he meant enough to me to make me break my virtual fast and eat a baked potato with cottage cheese and salad two days running, and that meant a lot. My weighing schedule was set for Sunday night, but I was so eager to find out what I'd lost that I weighed myself that morning when I got up.

Eight stones three!!! I hugged myself gleefully; in just a week, I'd lost ten pounds. In another two or three weeks, I'd get into the jeans, even if I kept my promise to Brad and ate proper diet meals of baked potatoes and chicken breasts.

Just as I got back from my afternoon run, Naomi's mother's car drew up outside our house. With a nasty sinking feeling, I went over to her.

"Where's Naomi?" she demanded, accusingly. "She told me she was staying with you this weekend."

"I—"

"Don't lie to me, Jo. I've already spoken to your mother. She hasn't seen Naomi for weeks. Where is she?"

Right then Naomi was, or should have been, on a train to London; after that, she had to get another one back here.

"She's gone to see a friend," I said. "She'll be back this evening."

"What friend? Where?"

I didn't like Mrs Moran's manner. It wasn't me who'd gone off on the dirty weekend. "All I know is she'll be back later," I said.

"But where has she been?"

I didn't tell her. She glared at me for a moment, and then with a gasp of exasperation she got into her car and drove off. I went indoors and called Rail Information. After an age, I found out when the train in Newquay arrived in London. I went to the station to meet Naomi, but she wasn't on the

London train that connected with the one from Newquay, or the next one.

Hope fading, I realized that she might have taken the bus, but when I went to the terminus, she wasn't there either. Despondently, I went back home.

Brad phoned from the hospital on his dinner break. "Hey, how's things?" he asked brightly.

I told him what had happened to Naomi. "That's tough," he said. Just then his beeper went off, so we finished the call.

I dialled Naomi's number, but her mother banged the phone down when she heard my voice.

I imagined the row that was going on at her house, and my heart ached for her.

Chapter 5

"It wasn't your fault," Naomi said, staring glumly into her cappuccino. "Katy phoned for some reason and Mum said I was at yours, so she phoned your house. When your mum said I wasn't there the silly bitch phoned Mum back and told her that."

It was Monday afternoon after work and Naomi only had fifteen minutes before she had to be home. Her parents are really primitive and they'd put her under a curfew for the entire summer, like she was some sort of criminal. Next thing, they'd get one of these electronic tags and make her wear it around her ankle.

"I hope I didn't get you into trouble as well."

I shook my head. "Mum was puzzled, that's all. She hasn't got a suspicious mind."

"You're lucky."

That's one way of looking at it, I thought. Both my parents are what you call goal orientated; as soon as they achieve one thing, they're off after the next. They expect Maddie and me to be like that too. It's not just GCSEs; it's A levels and then a good degree and, of course, a brilliant career after that. I slogged my guts out to get A-grade GCSEs but they didn't congratulate me, they just looked as if they'd expected as much.

I looked at Naomi. "Was it worth it?" I asked.

A dreamy expression came over her face. "Yes!" she said. "It was brill, mega, awesome! I don't know the words to describe it. I think it's love, Jo." Her face shaded. "He's asked me for next weekend, but I don't suppose I can make it now. He can't come up here, because he works Saturdays. But he said he can't wait for term to start, because then we can get together all the time."

She thought about it for a moment, stirring her coffee. "How's things with Brad?" I sipped my mineral water. "OK, but he's nagging me about my diet. He's worried I'll get anorexia."

Naomi laughed.

"I mean it," I said. "He told me he's got a sister and she's got it."

Naomi frowned. "I didn't know Brad had a sister."

"He has. She's six years older than him and she doesn't live at home. Apparently she got it in her first year at Uni. Ever since then, she's been in and out of hospital. It's really sad."

Naomi's eyebrows lifted. "Y'know, some boys

don't like their girlfriends being too attractive. They're scared they'll lose them."

"Brad's not like that," I said quickly.

"No? It's called co-dependency, Jo. It's when he wants you to have a fault, because it makes him feel more secure. He'd rather you didn't lose weight, because then you're not perfect and he can keep you in your place. I mean, you're not fat, but you'd be much more attractive if you were really slim. He probably thinks you'd go off with someone else."

"Brad's gorgeous. He could get anyone he wants."

"He's talent here, sure, but out in the real world there's lots of blokes that make him look like Mr Bean."

I gazed at her, wondered why she was so eager to put him down.

I began to doubt Naomi then. I wondered if despite her new boyfriend she was still jealous of me and Brad, but when I went home, I couldn't help thinking about what she'd said. Not about Brad looking like Mr Bean, but about him wanting me to be a little plump. He made such a fuss about my diet and all I was trying to do was to lose my spare tyre.

I needed to know what it feels like to go into a shop and try on a size eight; to know what it's like to look in a mirror without being ashamed. I wanted to know what it's like to pull up the zip on my jeans without a struggle; to be able to go out with Brad and sit down without constantly having to hold my stomach in, or folding my arms so that he can't see the fat.

Fat is gross. Fat is disgusting. It means you're selfish, gluttonous, you have no control. Like those women in supermarkets who waddle down the aisles, loading their carts with jam and bacon and sausages, sugar and cholesterol galore.

Food is the enemy. Maybe not food itself, but certainly all those food manufacturers who photo-graph Chocolate Pavlova to make it look like the Mona Lisa. They know it's unhealthy, they know fat kills people, but they keep on doing it to make a buck.

Food is seductive, as addictive as heroin. As I thought of a creamy tiramisu, I began to salivate. They say you get used to it after a while; after you've eaten healthy food you lose the urge for fat.

My stomach yawning, I went down to the kitchen, chopped carrots and leeks and broccoli and steamed it all with a little chicken stock. I ate a whole plateful and afterwards my stomach was full.

Maddie came back from Uni that week. Because of her course, she spent a month in Paris after the term ended, and before the next one begins, she's going to Brussels. That's supposed to be work?

She was working for Dad for six weeks, and just because she'd spent a year studying law, he paid her one and a half times what he paid me. But I wasn't jealous; Maddie's one of these people it's impossible to be jealous of. She's funny and kind, and she's always treated me as an equal, although I'm younger than her. If she weren't my big sister, she'd be my best friend.

I wanted to do something to celebrate her home-coming. I thought for a long time and the longer I thought, the more I thought about food. Maddie's got a thing about chocolate brownies, we both have – at least, I had until I started my diet. I'd seen this recipe in one of the Sunday supplements for a Chocolate Brownie Gâteau covered with ganache and chocolate flakes – total Death-on-a-Plate stuff, but if you ate it, at least you'd die happy.

Even the thought of it made me squirm with longing. On the day that Maddie was due to come home, I went to the supermarket and bought six hundred grams of chocolate and all the sugar, butter and cream that the recipe required. I then went home to make it.

As the chocolate began to melt, I began to count the calories. When I reached two thousand I stopped, and I was only about halfway through the list of ingredients!

The melting chocolate filled the kitchen with its smell. It looked dark and rich and delicious. I couldn't help it – I dipped my finger into the bowl and licked, then told myself off because the gâteau was Maddie's treat, it wasn't for me.

Feeling increasingly saintly, I melted butter and mixed it with the other things. I didn't even sneak a pecan. When I put the two layers of the cake into the oven, I felt positively martyr-ish.

As the layers baked, I made the ganache, which is a mixture of chocolate and double cream, and then I began to work the chocolate. The recipe called for the gâteau to be decorated with chocolate rolls, and to get the chocolate to do that you have to melt it and then manipulate it with a palette knife.

I was in heaven as I spread the melted chocolate on waxed paper and began to fold it back and fro. If you can't eat, then cooking is a really good substitute.

When the layers were ready, I took them out of the oven and left them to cool. Mum was supposed to come home early to cook Maddie's favourite dinner, which is roast pork with crackling and apple sauce, but I phoned her at the office and told her not to bother; I'd seen Gran doing it often enough.

As I chopped vegetables and peeled potatoes, I sang to myself; I hadn't felt so happy since Brad had told me that he was crazy about me.

I finished the gâteau just as Dad came home with Maddie, who he'd collected from the station. Maddie threw her arms around me. "Wow!" she exclaimed, as she saw my cake.

When Mum came home, we all sat down to dinner together. They were so engrossed in their pork that they didn't notice that I only ate vegetables. Afterwards I served the gâteau with great pride.

"Did you make that?" Dad asked.

I nodded.

"Maybe you should quit the firm and be our cook instead."

Maddie laughed. "We couldn't eat like this every night."

"We'd get terribly fat," Mum said.

I watched them eat.

"Aren't you having any?" Maddie asked.

I shook my head. "I kept on picking at it while I made it. I'm absolutely full."

Maddie groaned. "You must have some, Jo. You made it. It's not the same as picking bits."

"Come on, Jo, it's delicious," Mum said.

Dad said nothing. He just picked up a plate and cut me a slice.

I gazed at it. The brownie was so rich that it glistened and the ganache shone like burnished oak. The chocolate rolls on top shed paper-like flakes that fell like autumn leaves.

"Go on," Maddie said impatiently.

My hand shook as I picked up the fork. It hovered over the plate for a moment and then dropped down and gouged out a bite. I opened my mouth, felt the silky soft sensation of the mixture of cream and chocolate.

It really was a very good cake. I ate another bite and then another, and then it was finished and I was staring at the crumbs, which I picked up one by one.

"Want some more?" Maddie asked.

"It wouldn't be the same if we left it in the fridge," Dad said.

Maddie divided the remainder into four and gave us all a bit. I ate. I couldn't help it, I ate much quicker than the others, and when I was finished I sat watching them eat. If they weren't my family, I would've killed for that cake!

As they began to talk about Maddie's time in Paris, I slipped away. I went upstairs, where I stared at myself in the mirror in my bedroom. The capital M mocked me, as did the size eight jeans. I studied my reflection; I wasn't seeing myself as I was, but as I would be when the thousands of calories I had just eaten found their way to my hips.

I knew I'd never get into the jeans. I didn't deserve to, because I'd let myself go. I thought of all that food churning around my stomach, the fat being separated out by the digestive process and sent for storage. I imagined my veins and arteries clogging up with all the cholesterol.

I should feel sick, I told myself.

And then I realized that if I could actually *be* sick, I would lose it all.

I went to the bathroom and found an old tub of Epsom salts, all stuck together. I eased a lump out with my toothbrush, and drank it in a glass of water. When nothing happened, I drank another one.

I was trying to think of the vilest things imaginable, to force myself to throw up.

It didn't work at first.

I thought of my naked body, remembered Brad teasing me about my too-tight jeans. My stomach began to flutter. I knelt down by the toilet bowl and gagged, but nothing came up. Taking a deep breath, I pushed two fingers down my throat. I gagged again, dryly. I forced my fingers down my throat even deeper and then, at last, I was sick.

When it was over, I stared at the mess in the toilet bowl, and then I flushed it away. I was so ashamed of myself that I began to cry. I'd heard of girls doing that, and I'd always told myself that I never would.

I vowed to myself that I'd never do it again.

Maddie came into my room later that night. "How's it going, Splodge?"

I smiled wanly. Splodge is her nickname for me, a moniker I gained at the age of four because of my highly refined Impressionistic style in painting. It also described my puppy fat. I've given Maddie various nicknames over the years, but none of them has stuck to her in the way that mine has stuck to me.

"OK, I guess," I replied, propping myself up on one hand.

She looked around my room, at the big M and the jeans hanging on the front of my wardrobe.

"Motivation," I explained. "For once in my life, I'm determined to lose weight."

She looked me up and down. "I'd say you'd

done it already, sis. It was the first thing I noticed about you. I thought, Splodge is thin at last."

I pulled the waistband of my skirt. "I'm determined to get into size eight jeans."

"Wow! *Size eight jeans!* I swear to God, Splodge, I'll kill you if you do it. I'll never forgive you. I mean it."

I laughed to myself. Maddie is like me, big-boned, big-hipped. She was podgy too when she was at home, but since she's gone to Uni the weight's just dropped off. If she's not thin, at least she's fairly lean; I don't think the Gibson genes recognize the word "slim".

"How are you getting on with Paul?" I asked her.

Maddie's eyebrows lifted, and she sighed. "Jo, Paul's history. He's positively fossilized. Didn't I tell you about the new man in my life?"

I shook my head.

"Well, his name's Christian. He's French. He's doing an MBA. I met him at the beginning of last term, because he's doing his international marketing module over here. He's twenty-four, very brainy—"

"Is he as dreamy as he sounds?"

"Mmm hmm. And more! He's got green eyes and curly dark hair; his body's lean and mean, all muscle, no fat. I was staying with him in Paris. I'm still in shock, because I'm not going to be seeing him for six weeks. The thing is, he's just the nicest person, he's kind and considerate and his voice is just *so* sexy. So's the rest of him, when it comes to that."

I giggled. "Is it lurve?"

Maddie's eyes swivelled deliriously. "It might be, sis. It just might be. He was going back to Switzerland next term; he's at the European business school, but he's wangled it so he's doing his thesis here. We're going to get a flat together."

"*Wow!* That's just so cool."

"You won't tell them, Jo, will you? Mum might be OK about it, but I think that Dad would go ballistic at the thought of his daughter living with a Frenchman. He's five years older than me too. Dad'd probably say Christian's taking advantage or something crazy like that."

I shook my head.

"I mean, it's ridiculous. Christian's got a really good job, and he's got a bursary to do the course, so he's loaded — relatively speaking. If anyone's taking advantage of anyone, it's me taking advantage of him."

"I won't tell, Maddie," I said. "I'm really happy for you."

I meant it at the time. I really did.

Chapter 6

Thursday was Brad's day off. We couldn't meet up during the day, because I was working, but he met me in town later and we went ten-pin bowling. Afterwards, we wandered around for a bit. Although my jeans now felt loose, when I caught a glimpse of my reflection, I realized that I was still plump.

When we passed PJ's, Brad stopped. "You want a burger?"

I shook my head. "You shouldn't want one either," I said, "all that fat and cholesterol. It'll clog your veins, give you a heart attack by the time you're forty."

"OK," he said, "let's go for a Chinese instead."

"You're always hungry, Brad."

"Aren't you? It's well past dinner time."

"I ate before I came out."

"In the office?"

"Dad took me out for lunch," I lied. As usual, I'd

just had a couple of raw carrots and a cup of camomile tea.

In the restaurant, he ordered one of these specials – you know, about four different dishes and rice and noodles. As we waited for the food, I asked him how his flying was going.

"It's good," he said. "At least, I think it's good. I had the controls during take-off and although Jack's got an override, he didn't have to use it. I did most of the landing as well."

Jack is Brad's flying instructor. He's a crusty old ex-RAF pilot; he flew commercial jets for a while too before he got bored with it.

"Jack said that the BA course is over-subscribed by about two hundred to one." Brad paused and ran his hands through his hair. "I mean, with that many, how on earth do they choose the right ones? Jack says it's just luck. He says I should try the RAF. They'd jump at me."

"And what about your principles?"

Brad winced. "He told me to eat them."

As he went on about his woes, I watched a platter of rich, sweet, barbecued pork being delivered to the next table. The pungent aroma teased my nostrils, made my stomach yawn like a lion. Fleetingly, I thought that just one meal wouldn't hurt, before I reminded myself of the calories and the fat.

Brad was staring at me. I realized I was meant to respond to what he'd said, but I hadn't been listening.

I fidgeted with the tablecloth. "Sometimes you have to compromise," I said.

He shook his head. "I don't want to learn how to bomb people, or how to blow planes out of the sky."

"Maybe you could just fly mercy missions, like you could take food to Africa or someplace," I said hopefully. As soon as I mentioned the word *food* my stomach gaped like a hungry rhinoceros.

Brad shook his head again. "You can't join the RAF just to fly transports. If you join as a pilot, it's fast jet training, and that's fighters and bombers. You only get on to transports if you flunk at some stage. If you flunk the RAF, the airlines wouldn't touch you."

The food came: sweet and sour king prawns, beef in black bean sauce, lemon chicken and char sui pork. My mouth watered. Brad picked up a spoon and began to divide it evenly between our plates, one prawn for me and then one for him. As the pile on my plate grew, I told him I'd had enough, but he ignored me.

The scents of honey and spice and soy sauce mingled in my nostrils. I shifted in my seat and searched for a distraction. "You're assuming you won't get on to the BA course," I said. "That's not a foregone conclusion."

"It's a one-in-two-hundred chance. That's just about the same thing."

He began to eat. After a few mouthfuls, he looked quizzically at my untouched plate.

I speared a prawn, telling myself I wouldn't eat the batter, but it tasted so delicious that I finished it, batter and all. And another, and then another. In no time at all, I had eaten the lot.

I couldn't believe that it was gone, that my diet had lapsed yet again! If I'd only eaten the vegetables and a little rice, it would have been all right.

"You glutton!" I told myself in a murmur. "You greedy slob!"

"What's that?"

"Nothing," I said, rocking back on my chair, trying not to think about what I'd just done.

Brad smiled sadly. "Thanks for listening," he said.

The waiter came to remove the plates. Brad ordered banana fritters.

"I just hate the idea of killing anybody," he said, "but that's what the RAF trains you to do. If you want to be a pilot, it helps if you're a psychopath."

In my head, I was counting the calories in my stomach, imagining all that carbohydrate and fat heading straight for my hips.

As Brad began to list the reasons why war is futile, why fighting never achieves anything, all I could think of was little yellow fat cells expanding, engorging themselves with the vast meal I'd just eaten. It had been way over my daily quota by about a thousand calories or so, and I still hadn't managed to get into my size eight jeans.

". . . even the Second World War," Brad continued. "Sure, we had to fight Hitler, but we didn't stop the Holocaust."

Fat cells clump together in nodules, which are stored just under the skin of the stomach, bottom and thighs. As he talked, I could feel the nodules expanding. I couldn't concentrate on what he was saying.

"Excuse me," I said, as I got up and headed for the toilet.

Inside, I closed the door and knelt down by the bowl. I forced my fingers down my throat and held them there until I gagged. As I retched, I felt guilty, because I had promised myself that I wouldn't do it again.

But I had to, because of the fat. The most important thing in my life just then was getting rid of all those calories before they had a chance to become podge.

I was afraid that there was some food still left in my stomach, so I did it again, but only watery stuff came out.

Feeling awful, I washed my face quickly and dried it with loo paper, and then I went back to Brad.

He was still preoccupied; his expression told me that he was somewhere very far away, maybe in the cockpit of a BA Concorde. I knew he was afraid that it would only ever be a dream.

He looked so wistful, so vulnerable, that my heart ached for him. I felt really awful because I'd been thinking of myself, not him.

We left the restaurant to walk home.

"Y'see, I'm going to do the BA aptitude tests soon," he said, as he put his arm around me.

"Oh," I replied, lamely. I was wondering what I could say to help him, but all that stuff about if you want something enough you'll get it just doesn't work in the real world. And I had other things on my mind, like if I lost another few pounds I would finally be able to get into the jeans.

"I'm sorry for going on about it."

"It's OK," I said, "I understand. I mean, I know how much it means to you. But I think you'll make it, I really do."

Brad's arm tightened around me. "If I don't, will you stick around?"

"Of course! You've got to believe in yourself, Brad. You'll make it someway or another. I'm pretty sure of that."

"And if I don't. . ."

"You'll still be Brad."

"I don't want to fail, Jo. I don't know how to cope with it."

I shivered. The idea of failure terrified me. Even the thought of it gave me goose pimples. I'd never failed at anything, but then I'd never really tried something that was really difficult. I could just see the expressions on the faces of my parents, if I, Jo Gibson, became the first true failure in the mighty Gibson clan.

I just couldn't bear it. I'd die with shame.

"Hey!" Brad said. "You look like you've seen a ghost."

I smiled, tried to shrug the fear away. "I just think you're very brave to try," I said, knowing that I was not and never would be.

"That's all I can do," Brad said.

We walked in silence for a while.

"I'm working this weekend," Brad said, as we turned into my road, "but I've got next Thursday off. My folks are away; they're going to see Lucy. Dad's got something to do in London, so they're staying overnight. We'd have the place to ourselves."

"Umm," I mumbled.

"We don't have to do anything you don't want to do," he said quickly.

We reached my house.

"I'll call you tomorrow," Brad said.

"OK."

He kissed me. I smiled as he left, but inside I was shaking.

I rushed indoors and then up to the bathroom, where I weighed myself.

Seven stones, ten pounds. I was trembling with relief as I saw that I hadn't put on anything; in fact, in a couple of days, I'd lost four pounds.

This diet was the most difficult thing I'd ever done in my life. I just had to make it work, had to get into those size eight jeans.

If I didn't, I'd never forgive myself.

Chapter 7

Right then, I was perched on the edge of a precipice. If I'd pulled back, I would have been OK, but I didn't, I went on and then, once I was over the edge, it was too late.

My life was about to spiral way out of control.

It didn't feel like madness at the time, and in a way, it wasn't. I didn't hear voices in my head, or see things that weren't there. I didn't have delusions, I didn't think I was God or the devil, I didn't mutter to myself in the street and I was never, ever violent.

But it was a kind of madness none the less, because I began to lose touch with reality. The world I lived in changed: I began to realize that I had enemies everywhere. Everybody I cared about wanted me to keep on being Jo the Fattie. Nobody understood me, nobody at all.

My world was cold and harsh and grey; all colour was muted and sounds were distant; there was no happiness or even contentment. There was just one focal point in my life: the overwhelming compulsion to be thin and to stay thin, nothing else mattered. Not my family nor my friends, not even Brad, although a while passed before I realized that.

There was something wrong with me, and the only way to put it right was to get rid of the fat that clung to me in clumps like leeches, sucking my life and happiness away.

On Saturday morning I got up. Before I did anything else, I weighed myself. I didn't even drink any camomile tea because I knew that would add an ounce or two until the water had passed through my system. Then I showered and went back to my bedroom, where I took the size eight jeans off the hanger.

The cardboard label was still stapled to the waistband. That was really the point of no return, because the shop where I had bought them had a policy of unconditional refunds so long as you brought whatever it was back unworn within a month.

I stared at it for a long time before I unpicked the staples and removed the label. They weren't Levi's, they didn't cost so much, but they were size eight jeans nevertheless.

I only ever wear Levi's normally but I'd been so unsure of myself that I hadn't wanted to risk the extra cash.

Very slowly, I sat down and began to put them on. The jeans slid over my legs easily, and then tightened slightly over my thighs. Breathing in, I stood up and pulled. The waistband hesitated at my hips; I pulled a little more and then it was over them.

I did up the button and the zip. I couldn't believe it.

I, Jo Gibson, was wearing size eight jeans!

Maddie wasn't up yet. Christian had phoned last night, and she'd still been talking to him when I went to bed. I burst into her room.

"Look!" I said.

Maddie opened her eyes groggily. "What is it?"

I preened. "Size eight jeans," I replied.

She sat up in bed. "Oh, wow! That's just brilliant, Jo! What does it feel like?"

"Pretty good." I was turning from side to side in front of her mirror, studying myself. Even though I was wearing size eight jeans, my hips still looked thicker than they should be. "The only thing is, they're not Levi's. They're cheapo imitations."

Maddie yawned. "Take them back and change them for Levi's."

"I can't. I've taken the label off."

"They won't mind. I'll come with you if you like."

She got up, rubbing her eyes. "You look terrific, Jo. It's got to be one of life's great experiences, wearing size eight jeans."

In town, we went to the jeans shop, where I

swapped the cheapo pair for Levi's. I put them on in the changing room and put the pair I'd been wearing into the carrier bag. I'd give them to Oxfam later; I'd certainly never wear size 12 again. Then we mooched around the mall for a bit, window shopping.

In the window of one shop I saw a top that would be just right for my new jeans. It was very tight and figure-hugging, the kind of thing you couldn't wear if you had so much as an ounce of fat.

"Let's go in," Maddie said. "You can try it on."

Inside, it was just an amazing feeling to be looking at the small end on the rails. Maddie found the top and we went off to the changing room.

I put it on. I wasn't too sure of it, because it seemed that the fabric clung too closely to my spare tyre. It reminded me that I still had to lose some more.

"It makes me look fat," I said.

Maddie swooned in mock-horror. "Fat? Kiddo, you're a size eight!"

I plucked at the flesh around my waist.

"That's fat."

"Jo! It's loose skin, that's all. If you go to the gym and exercise a bit, it'll tighten up in no time."

I looked at the ticket. "I can't afford it."

"I can," Maddie said. "Call it an early birthday present. Call it guilt, because Dad's paying me fifty quid a week more than he's paying you."

That's my sister. She's so nice, it's impossible to

fall out with her. It's also impossible to be jealous of her, although she's got a dreamy boyfriend, a great bod and a brilliant mind.

With me diffidently wearing my new top, we wandered out of the shop to the coffee bar. Maddie bought cappuccinos and two chocolate fudge cheesecakes.

"Whoa," I said, as she plonked the stratospherically calorific concoction in front of me. It wasn't just cheesecake, it was cheesecake slathered with cream and chocolate flakes.

"To celebrate being a size eight," Maddie said.

"I won't be size eight if I eat things like that."

"Loosen up, Jo. You've made it. You don't need to diet any more."

My treacherous stomach was groaning with need.

Maddie looked at me. "Go ahead, Jo. What's wrong with you?"

I picked up the fork and began to eat, trying to take as little as I could. With each bite, I could feel the waistband of the jeans tightening. The same old battle was going on, but this time I could sense victory – the cheesecake just didn't taste the same as it used to.

Maddie frowned.

"I've been off fat for so long, I guess my tastes have changed," I said, as I pushed the uneaten part aside. I just knew that if I ate it I'd have to be sick.

Maddie's frown lasted for a moment longer, then

she shrugged. "When am I going to meet Superman?" she asked.

My face went hot. So far, I'd avoided Brad's encounter with the Gibson inquisition, but Maddie had seen him from the window and she'd been nagging me ever since.

I flexed my arms. "Soon. It's not you, Madds, it's them."

She winced. "I know what you mean."

"Y'know what Dad's like. It's all about, 'I hope your intentions are honourable, young man', and stuff like that. I mean, they're OK in theory, but in practice Dad is like a caveman. When that boy took me home after Naomi's party, he subjected him to the third degree. And he wasn't even my boyfriend. We'd just got off together, sort of."

"Brad's different, huh?"

"How d'you mean?"

"I mean, he *is* your boyfriend. You've been with him for a while, haven't you?"

"Yeah. It's been good so far, but. . ." I shrugged.

"But what?"

"I don't know, Maddie. I keep on thinking he'll change his mind about me."

"Why?"

"Well, for example, we haven't actually . . . you know . . . yet, but I'm worried that if he sees me naked, he'll go, 'yuk!' "

Maddie laughed.

"I mean, Sly Stallone's got bigger breasts than I have, and I've got the haunches of a quarterback."

"Jo! You're a size eight, for heaven's sake. You've got a great personality and a beautiful face. He's lucky to have you. He's not putting you under pressure or anything?"

I shook my head. "No. Nothing like that. Brad's cool. He's new-mannish, in a way. It's just that I know he's thinking about it. I know that he wants to and it makes me feel guilty, because I'm not sure."

"Don't feel guilty, Jo. You only lose your virginity once."

"I don't want to lose him, Madds."

"You won't. At least, not because of that. Gran's not often right, but she's right when it comes to that. If you mean enough to him, he'll wait for you."

"But what if I don't?"

"You'll lose him anyway. That's life, kiddo. You can't change it. But that's only if he's an SOB, and it doesn't sound like he is."

She stirred a couple of sugar lumps into her cappuccino; I took mine straight. It was only sixty calories or so; I'd just have to live with it.

"What d'you think about the great Gibson summer hols?" she asked.

I frowned. "What?"

"Of course, you don't know," she said. "They were talking about it on Thursday when you were out. They want to go to Singapore and Indonesia for the last week in August and the first week in September."

"I thought we weren't going anywhere because of that case Dad's got."

"Apparently it's under control. Mum said she'd ask you, but I said I thought you'd be thrilled, because you've always wanted to go to the Far East."

I moaned. "I'm supposed to be going to Spain with Brad. There's a whole gang of us going together. I told Mum ages ago and she said it was OK."

Maddie swore in French. "She must have forgotten. I'm not going either. Christian and I might be going away somewhere, but as far as they're concerned, I'm going to Brussels two weeks early."

"They wouldn't mind if you told them the truth."

"Maybe not, but it feels kind of strange, telling your father that you're going on hols with your boyfriend. I'll tell Mum, but not him."

I rested my chin on my hand. "I'll tell them when I get back home," I said. "They won't mind so long as you're around to watch over me."

"But I won't be here," Maddie hissed.

"They won't know that."

"When's Gran coming back?"

"Not until October. The ticket cost so much, she thinks it'd be a waste to come back before then."

We giggled.

Maddie sat back and looked around. "Oh, lord!" she said. "There's Sarah Evans."

I followed her eyes and saw an old friend of hers.

Maddie leaned closer. "I was supposed to ring her when I got back, but I forgot."

Just then, Sarah saw her. She waved and then made her way over to our table. I stood up to give her my seat, because there were just two.

"I'll see you later," I said, as they began to talk.

I wandered around a little more, and then I left the mall to head home. On the way, I passed Breeze. I could see Naomi through the window, talking to the other girls who worked there.

They all looked impossibly slim, I felt gross just looking at them but then I remembered that I was wearing size eight jeans.

I was about to walk away when Naomi looked up and saw me. She waved and then she came to the door.

"Hi, Jo," she said.

I stood up straight so that she could see I'd lost weight, but she didn't seem to notice. "Wanna come in?" she asked. "There's no customers this early. You can try on some of the clothes if you like."

I followed her inside. You felt the difference as soon as you walked through the door. Even the air smelt expensive. The shop was done up in what they call minimalist chic, but the light oak floor was polished to a high sheen and the fittings were arranged like sculptures. There weren't nearly so many clothes as there are in other shops, but I supposed that was because the stuff in Breeze cost ten times as much.

Naomi waved her hand airily as she ran off a list of designer names.

I was almost afraid to touch, but my mouth watered. It felt like being in Aladdin's Cave. Naomi began to show me things: T-shirts that cost sixty-five pounds a pop and *the* sandal, of the summer – a couple of bands of burnished leather that came to over two hundred pounds.

She kept on asking me if I wanted to try things on. I refused until she showed me the most glorious dress. It was a little sliver of silk scattered with occasional sequins that danced with the light. It sounds tacky, I know, but believe me, it was not. The sequins were transparent; they didn't look like sequins but somehow they made the dress come alive.

I held it up against me and sighed.

"Go on," Naomi said.

I went into the changing room, for once not nervous of taking my clothes off. I put the dress on without looking in the mirror, but when I saw my reflection even I knew that I looked good.

Naomi came through. "The clogs put a damper on it," she said.

I slipped them off.

"I'd die happy if I could have this dress!"

"Come through," she said. "The light's better in the shop."

I followed her and pirouetted in front of a mirror. The dress clung to every curve of my body; it would be just perfect if I lost the fat that still stuck to my lower half.

The other assistants clustered around, telling me how good it looked.

I glanced at the label and nearly fainted. This tiny dress cost seven hundred and ninety-five pounds!

I should have taken it off, but it had cast its spell around me so I pirouetted some more.

"Why's it so much?" I asked Naomi in a whisper.

She shrugged. "That's nothing for a designer dress."

"But who can afford it?"

"You'd be surprised."

One of the other girls laughed. "Hookers. Drug dealers."

We giggled.

"You really do look good in it," she said, "like it was made for you."

"Well, could it be made to follow me home? I can't afford it, but I'm sure I could find it wardrobe room."

We giggled some more, and then suddenly everybody stopped. I looked around and saw a very tall, dark man staring at me. He was the James Bond type; his face was deeply tanned and angular and his teeth were a brilliant white.

"That's Simon," Naomi whispered, "the owner."

He walked straight up to me. "Well, hello!" he said.

"H . . . hello," I mumbled, my throat tight.

He held his hand out. "I'm Simon."

I shook his hand; my hand felt hot and sweaty in

his cool one and I saw the glint of a diamond ring on his finger.

"I'm Jo. I'm a friend of Naomi's," I babbled. "I just came in to buy myself a birthday present. I love this dress, but I'd better go and take it off. I mean, I can't afford it. I wish I could, but I can't."

He was walking around me in a circle, like he was a tiger and I was a lamb.

"Don't take it off just yet," he said.

Goosebumps formed on my arms as I felt his scrutiny. I stood very still, trying not to tremble.

Nobody spoke. Everything was motionless, suspended in time like the moment before a thunderclap.

Simon continued to circle me, I felt his piercing gaze like a surgeon's knife. I held my stomach in, praying that he would not see my flab.

Someone came into the shop and the spell was broken. The girls moved away, but Simon did not.

"I'll just go and change," I said.

"Not so fast," he replied. "Why don't you come to work here? I'm always looking for girls like you."

I blanched. Was he blind? Couldn't he see that I wasn't like the other girls? Didn't he notice my minute breasts, or the fat that clung to my hips and thighs?

"Tell you what," he said, "if you do come to work here, I'll give you a discount on that dress."

"I don't know," I mumbled. "I'm at sixth-form college with Naomi, but I've been working for my dad."

"It's much more fun to work here. I pay very well, you know."

I was thinking that the only way out of it would be to buy the dress. Dad's given me a credit card for emergencies, but I wasn't sure that this would count.

Simon came closer and flicked a stray strand of hair away from my eyes. His eyes were dark brown flecked with grey and I could see the stubble on his chin. His after-shave smelled of autumn woods.

"What d'you say, Jo? It would be such a pity if you never wore that dress again."

I swallowed. My throat still felt very tight. I was afraid but at the same time I was elated. Just weeks ago, I'd never have dared cross this door, but here I was being offered a job by the owner of the coolest shop for miles around.

Even if I was still a little flabby, I was on the way to losing it. And Dad wouldn't mind if I left the firm; he'd probably just given me a job because I'm his daughter.

"OK," I croaked.

"Good. Come in Monday morning. We don't open till ten, but if you come at nine-thirty Carin will kit you out."

"OK," I said again.

His eyes followed me as I walked to the changing room. "See you Monday," he said.

After I'd changed, I put the dress back on its hanger and I handed it back to Naomi.

She took it brusquely. "Simon's like that with every girl he meets," she said. "Don't go getting any ideas about him."

Chapter 8

In the end, I didn't start at Breeze that week. When I told Dad I was going to leave his firm, he asked me to stay until I'd finished sorting out the files for the motorway extension case. I was annoyed but also a bit chuffed, because I knew he was pleased with the work I'd done. And the extra week gave me a little more time to get rid of that fat.

When I phoned Simon on Monday morning, he just said, "That's cool, Babes," in a voice that sent a shiver down my spine. Not because I fancied him – because I didn't – but because it sounded as if *he* might fancy *me*.

Things were OK at home. I was cooking most of the family meals and I always made a totally calorific pudding. My parents were so busy that they didn't notice that I wasn't eating much. Despite the promise I'd made to Brad, some days I ate nothing at all.

Maddie was working hard; she spent most of the

rest of her time thinking about Christian or talking to him on the phone.

When we did eat together, I made a point of gorging myself on salady stuff; I didn't want her to start going on again about me not needing to diet any more.

On Thursday, as we'd agreed, Brad picked me up from Dad's office. He was exhilarated because he'd just come back from a flying lesson and this time he'd both taken off and landed on his own. He was going to do his BA aptitude tests in a couple of weeks and he was hoping he'd be able to show them his flight log with that in it. Jack had told him that he would be ready to go solo soon.

I was thrilled for him, but I was terrified that he would fail the tests. It wasn't that I didn't believe in him, because I did, I knew he could do it, but I worried that something silly would go wrong, like his car would break down, or he'd get lost in the tangle of roads around Heathrow.

That's what would probably happen to me if I had to go to something as important as that.

"How's Lucy?" I asked as we walked home. The conversation had flagged, and I had to search my mind for something to say. There were butterflies in my stomach at the thought of being alone with him – not pleasant ones, but fear that he'd nag me about my diet again. And, of course, there was the old ever-present fear that if he – or any other boy – saw my naked body, he'd be turned off.

I was almost envious of Lucy, in a way. At least she knew what it was like to *really* lose weight.

The fact was, I was still fat. I spent a lot of time studying my body. No matter which way I looked, I was podgy around my hips and thighs. Although the scales told me that I was losing weight consistently at the rate of about a pound every two days, the mirror told a different story.

The scales were wrong, I was sure. When I'd started my diet, although I looked thinner, they told me I'd lost no weight at all, and now they were telling me that I *was* losing weight, even though I could see the fat.

I was beginning to despair. The fat clung on to me like a leech, my own personal albatross. I thought I would've been all right when I got down to about seven and a half stones, but I was seven stone three pounds and I *still* had a lot of flab. I'd changed my target weight to six and a half stones. Surely to goodness that would be enough!

Brad's face was fretted with worry lines. "She's actually been a bit better," he replied. "She was in hospital for months – I mean another hospital. She's been in about half a dozen so far. We were really worried that when she got out she'd just go back to her old ways, but she goes for counselling twice a week and so far, she's sticking to it. She's still thin, but she's eating properly. She's thinking of going back to finish her degree in October."

"That's good."

"I hope so. Thing is, my parents blame themselves."

"Why?"

"Lucy was born the year Mum graduated. My grandparents took care of her for the first few years because Dad was still training and they decided that Mum would work until he qualified. They didn't have much money. Lucy came to stay with us when I was born. They feel really guilty because they think they neglected her."

"Did they?"

He shook his head vigorously. "I don't think so. She's six years older than me so we've never been that close. She was fine until she left home. It all started at Uni. I thought it was funny at first – I was only twelve and I just didn't understand. Lucy was really emaciated, but she wouldn't eat. Mum gave up her job to take care of her, but she got worse. And then when we moved here, Lucy wouldn't come. For a while it looked like Dad was going to have to quit his job because of her, but the doctor who was treating her then told him to move anyway because he was making her worse by pandering to her. He said it was all to do with Lucy not wanting to grow up. In the end, we moved here and Lucy shared a flat with some girls at college, but they were doing fashion and they were all on diets so Lucy just got worse. She's been in intensive care a couple of times, once because she was starving herself and once because she tried to kill herself.

"It's really horrible, Jo. It's not just Lucy, it's the whole family. It's like there's this big black cloud hovering over us all the time. She's my sister and I love her, but sometimes I just get so angry with her. The way she behaves is so selfish. She doesn't realize what she's doing to us."

"Mmm," I said. "And your father lost his job anyway."

We reached his house. He opened the gate and we walked to the door.

"It's been grim," he said, as he opened the door, "but it's getting better now."

The butterflies in my stomach had become angry wasps now that I was alone with him.

Once we were inside, Brad didn't stop. He went through the back door to the garden, where a barbecue was glowing on the patio.

I looked up at the sullen sky.

"It was nice earlier," he said.

Beneath my sweater, I could feel goosebumps forming. I was always cold these days. He lifted the grill with tongs and extracted two foil wrapped baked potatoes, then he went inside and came back with a plate of thick Cumberland sausages.

"It's really hot, so it won't take long," he said, as he put them on the grill. "Wanna Coke while we wait?"

"OK."

He got the drinks, then he sat down on one of the loungers while I took the other one. I was shaking.

"Relax," he said.

The sausages were beginning to cook, throwing off a smell that teased my nostrils. I blinked and reminded myself of the fat.

"I told them you were coming round."

"Oh?"

"We've got this neighbour, Miss Clark. She's a retired headmistress and she's a right old bat."

I laughed. "I know; I remember her from school. I didn't realize she lived around here."

"She does, worse luck! She's always either in her garden or looking out her window. Whatever she's doing, she's actually watching everything that goes on. She lives right next door and she knows my parents are away, so she would've told them when she saw me turning up with you."

"It's weird. I can't imagine Miss Clark doing anything but giving really boring lessons and telling people off. We used to think that she was a vampire – not a normal vampire, because she came out during the day instead of the night, but we were pretty sure that she wasn't actually human."

Brad smiled. "She certainly is, though I wish she wasn't. She's the street's version of MI5 and GCHQ, all rolled into one."

There was a rustle at the hedge and then Miss Clark peered over, her half-moon glasses perched on the end of her nose.

"Oh, it's you, Bradley," she said, before her

gaze turned to me. "Jo Gibson, isn't it? How are you, my dear?"

I gulped. She'd never called me that at school. Only Joanna or, occasionally, *you silly little girl*! "I'm fine, Miss Clark. How are you?"

"I'm managing, dear, although I wish the weather was a bit better. Hopefully the sun will shine tomorrow. They do keep on about global warming, but it's been chilly all week. I suppose the water company will be glad of the drizzle. Oh, well, I suppose I'd better get back to my roses."

Her head dipped down. Brad stood up on tiptoe, then he held his finger to his mouth.

"The old bat's just the other side of the fence," he hissed.

We both collapsed into silent giggles. He turned the sausages, then went into the kitchen and came back with a radio, which he turned on. He began to hum to himself, then he scratched his head.

"Pray for rain," he whispered. "That way, we've got an excuse to go back indoors."

"When are you going to see BA?" I asked him.

"A week on Tuesday. It's near the airport, so I'm borrowing Mum's car. It lasts all day. It's supposed to be aptitude tests, but I don't have the foggiest what it's going to be like."

The rustle of garden shears came over the fence. We were both terribly aware of the old lady on the other side of it.

"It'll just be a load of questions," I said. I know something about assessment, because Mum's a personnel director. "To find out if you've got the right personality to be a pilot, and so on."

Brad frowned. "What's that?"

"It's probably to do with being decisive and having leadership qualities – how you get on with people and things like that. I wouldn't worry, Brad. That's you to a T."

Brad grunted. "Thanks a lot, Jo!"

"Come on, Brad. You're not exactly the shy and retiring type."

"I'll be really nervous when I get there."

"They know that, Brad. They expect it. Part of it will be about how you handle it even though you're really nervous. That's a good test of your nerves, which you need if you're going to be a pilot. I know you: you'll be nervous at first but then you'll get into it. You'll make a success of it; I'm sure you will."

"What if my nerves get the better of me?"

"They won't. They never have in the past."

He shook his head. "There's so much riding on this, Jo."

I trembled at the thought. "I know," I said, "but I also know that you've got what it takes.

"I mean, I've never even *flown* on a BA plane. When we go on holiday, it's always some cheapo charter. I've never even been on a 747, and half their fleet is 747s."

"That's got nothing to do with it. Just think how much you know about planes. Remember how well you've done at your lessons. Jack's backing you, and I don't think he would if he didn't think you'd be able to make it."

Brad went inside and came back with some rolls, which he put on the grill to toast. Then he fetched a big bowl of salad and we sat down to eat the food.

The sausage looked delicious, but I couldn't bear to eat it. It was full of fat, and I didn't want to have to make myself sick again. So I filled my plate with salad, which I ate slowly as Brad wolfed down his food.

When he'd finished, he looked at my sausage and roll, which I hadn't touched. I hadn't touched the baked potato either, but I'd squidged it around so that it looked as if I had.

"Jo!" he said, exasperated.

I squirmed in my seat. "I haven't eaten meat for ages. I'm virtually vegetarian."

He sighed. I helped myself to more salad in a effort to distract him.

"Why didn't you tell me?"

"You never asked."

He took my sausage and roll and ate it himself, then he went back to the kitchen and plonked a carton of ice-cream on the table.

"Häagen Dazs!"

My stomach twisted into a knot. "I'm so full already," I said. "I've had heaps of salad."

He ignored me and spooned the ice-cream into two bowls. I toyed with mine when he ate his, but when his eyes lifted I spooned a little into my mouth. I had to, else he'd ask why not.

It was ecstatic, orgasmic, incredibly good! The sensation made me feel dizzy and all gooey inside. I took another spoonful and then another, telling myself that it was OK, I'd just have to make myself sick again.

And then it was finished. It just wasn't enough. I could have eaten another bowlful, another ten bowlfuls, if it came to that. I shivered with delight at the thought that I could eat as much ice-cream as I liked, so long as I made myself sick afterwards.

"That was good," I said.

Brad grinned at me. "I'm glad you enjoyed it. I was really worried when you didn't eat your sausage. That was the kind of thing that Lucy used to do."

I smiled.

When he took the dishes into the kitchen, I went to help. The radio was still playing outside, so, with luck, the old bat would think that we were still there.

Brad washed the dishes and I dried. When he finished, his arms closed around me. He kissed me softly on my neck, and it felt good. I closed my eyes and let myself relax against him. His hands ran down my sides.

"You've lost weight," he said.

"Only a little bit."

"Don't, Jo."

I was thinking that I had to get away soon; I had to make myself sick.

"Don't what, Brad?"

"Don't lose any more weight, Jo. You don't need to." He spun me around and looked deep into my eyes. "I mean it, Jo. You're thin enough already."

"I'm fine, Brad, Stop pestering me about it. You're worrying too much. You think just because Lucy got anorexia, I'm going to get it too, but I won't. I promise you."

"Really truly?"

"Cross my heart and hope to die."

He lifted my chin with his hands. "I couldn't bear it if that happened to you, Jo. I mean it. I just couldn't."

I smiled. "You won't have to, because it won't."

He kissed me. I really enjoyed it at first, then it stopped feeling good. I was so desperate to get to the bathroom and make myself sick before all that fat got into my system. Then I started to worry because if I broke off, he might take it the wrong way.

It was weird, the way I felt about Brad. Sometimes I didn't want to see him, like I didn't want to eat with him because he always pestered me, but when I wasn't with him, I was thinking about him. (When I wasn't thinking about my diet, that is.) It was for him that I needed to lose all the weight, because I just knew that he wouldn't love me if I was fat. At least, he was a big part of the reason. The other part was for myself, because I really hated myself when I saw that flab. It meant that I had no self control, no will-power, that I might *fail*.

Just as I began to panic, the phone rang. Brad broke off to answer it, but he took it on the kitchen phone.

I sighed. I was going to head for the loo, but I didn't want to make it too obvious. He said "OK" a couple of times, then put the receiver back.

"That was Dad," he said. "They're at the station. They're bringing Lucy back."

"Is she OK?" I asked anxiously.

"She's great, apparently. She's coming home for the weekend and then she's going back next week. Dad just said he didn't want to disturb us." He grinned sheepishly.

"I'd better go."

"No. Stay and meet Lucy."

I shook my head. I didn't want to intrude. Besides, if I hurried home, I could be sick in the bathroom there without Brad or anyone else knowing anything about it.

Chapter 9

When I started at Breeze, Carin, the manageress, gave me an outfit to wear. It was these really slick Italian trousers with a printed net top. It was just so cool! When I looked in the mirror, I didn't believe it was me.

The trousers were size eight, but the cut was so slim that I couldn't put on even an ounce in weight. The flab around my waist was very obvious.

"You look fine," Carin said, as I gazed at my reflection. "You've got to look good, but not so good that you'll make the customers on edge about how they look themselves." She was really friendly as she showed me the various designers' collections and how to use the till and the credit card machine. "The main thing is, you have to make them feel at ease," she said. "Don't ever let them think that you're pressurizing them into a sale. Just be yourself, Jo."

I smiled nervously.

Naomi was standing with the other girls. As Carin left to go back to the office, Naomi's eyes followed her.

"It's really sad," she said.

"What is?"

"She's madly in love with Simon, but he treats her like dirt." She shook her head. "Carin's so crazy about him that she just lets him do it."

I felt a pang because I hated to hear of anyone being treated like that, especially someone as nice as Carin. Although I didn't want to admit it to myself, Simon fascinated me in a strange sort of way.

Naomi folded her arms. There was a knowing look in her eyes. "You have to know how to handle a man like that." She finished the nail she was buffing and started on the next one. "How's Brad?"

"Good. He's going for tests for the BA pilot training scheme next week."

"I hate to tell you this, Jo, but I saw him with someone else the other day."

My stomach dived. "Oh?"

"'Fraid so. She's really beautiful. She has long auburn hair and amazing legs. She's almost as tall as he is."

I laughed in relief. "Naomi, that's his sister! She came home for the weekend."

Naomi studied her perfect nails; there was a disappointed look on her face. I was disappointed too, because I knew our friendship was over and there was nothing I could do about it. Naomi had changed, had become someone that I didn't particularly want to know.

Maybe working at Breeze wasn't such a good idea after all, I thought.

A customer came in, but nobody did anything. We all tried to look busy as she wandered around the shop, studying the rails. When she found something she liked, one of the girls went over and took her into a changing room.

She left fifteen minutes later, poorer by £499.95. Or rather, since she'd paid with a gold American Express Card, maybe I should say "less rich".

"Easy sale," Naomi said. "She's one of our regulars."

"Is it always like that?"

"Nope," said Lallie, one of the other girls. "Some of them are really nervous when they come in, and you have to put them at ease. You just have to play it by ear."

I wondered what it would be like to be able to spend five hundred pounds on a dress, just like that.

As the days passed, I got more used to the idea, although I knew I would never get completely used to it. I watched the different customers come in and how the girls reacted and I began to learn how to judge when to approach a customer, or whether to approach them at all. I even managed a couple of sales myself, though they weren't particularly difficult ones. The thing was, some of the customers really couldn't afford the clothes. They'd come in diffidently, saying they only had one hundred and fifty pounds to spend, or whatever, then one of the more experienced assistants would take over and persuade them to spend at least double that. They'd take an outfit in when the customer was in the changing room and then they'd tell the customer to come out and have a proper look at themselves while we all stood around oohing and ahing.

It almost always worked, but I felt guilty about it.

Brad was working every day at the hospital up to the day of his interview, which he was taking off. He was on late shifts, and we used to meet at the coffee shop in the mall at lunchtime. He sometimes tried to make me eat something, but I used to tell him that I'd had a sandwich at work, and he was so distracted that he didn't make any more of it.

Sometimes, I was sure that I was falling in love with him. At other times I resented him, even actively disliked him, because in a way, he had become my conscience – that inner voice that told me that I was eating so little that sooner or later I would make myself ill.

But that inner voice was fading. As the days passed and my weight slowly crept down, I was sure that it would soon be over, and I would have lost the last of my flab.

But although my weight had gone below seven stones, my stomach, hips and thighs stayed fat. And the other benefit I'd expected didn't happen either: my breasts were still miniscule. I'd hoped that as I lost weight, they'd begin to look larger compared to the rest of me.

Brad was really keyed up about the coming tests, and I was doing my best to reassure him. Several times I asked my mother for advice, but I didn't actually introduce him to her even though she could have helped him a lot. For some reason that I didn't understand at the time, I just did not want Brad and my parents to get together.

Now I know what it was, but then I put it down to coyness. As I've said, Dad is truly a Neanderthal when it comes to boys.

On the day before his aptitude tests, Brad flew solo for the first time. He was elated when he phoned me later to tell me about it. But he was also terribly afraid that he'd muff the tests by making a silly mistake.

As I put the phone down, I was really frightened that I might have helped him to fail because I hadn't let him talk to my mother. She could have helped him so much. She's got a degree in psychology and she knows all about aptitude tests. There was really no reason not to ask for her help, beyond that desire I had to keep Brad and my parents apart.

And that was just pure selfishness.

I prayed that night, for the first time in years. And then I cried with shame, because I hadn't done my best for him.

On the day of the interview, I began to feel Brad's

jitters in the morning. By lunchtime I was a nervous wreck, pacing the floor as I tried to still the tremors in my hands.

"What's the matter?" Carin asked.

"It's my boyfriend. He's doing aptitude tests for pilot training today. It means the world to him, y'know?"

Carin nodded understandingly.

"I can't help worrying."

Naomi yawned. "Won't you be more worried if he gets the job? All these dreamy air hostesses. . ."

"They're called cabin crew now," I snapped. How dare she voice my innermost fear!

Carin stood up. "C'mon. You can help me mark down stuff for the sale. There's about a hundred T-shirts we have to get rid of."

I spent the afternoon steam-pressing tired old clothes – dead stock, as Carin called it.

I'd arranged to meet Brad in the juice bar at six, but when I got there, there was no sign of him. I waited anxiously for an hour, all sorts of dreadful scenarios drifting through my mind. It would take him at least an hour to drive back from Heathrow, but he should have finished at about half-past four, so he should have been there on time.

I wondered if he'd really muffed it and was driving around somewhere in despair. I even thought about suicide, but Brad wasn't the type. Pilot training means everything to him, but if this didn't work, he'd find another way of getting there.

Even though he's wanted to fly for BA since he

was old enough to think, somehow he'd get over it.

But would I? If I'd taken him to see Mum, he would have had a much better chance of getting through the tests. Just as I was beginning to contemplate suicide myself, he turned up.

He was flushed and excited, gabbling at three hundred words a minute.

"Hey, slow down!" I said, thrilled because I could sense it hadn't been the absolute disaster I'd feared.

He took a deep breath. "I'm really starving, Jo. D'you mind if we go somewhere where I can eat some real food?"

I laughed as we walked over to PJ's. As he ordered a double bacon cheeseburger with fries and potato skins and a chocolate shake, I said I'd had a salad in the juice bar.

A lie, but it was only a little one, and if it wasn't quite white, it was the palest shade of ivory.

"So what happened?"

"Well, I got there. There was about twenty of us – it was a bit like doing A levels again. It was tough at first, but when I got the hang of it it was OK. I keep on thinking I made a muck of it, but I've got a good feeling, you know? At least, I managed to let them know that I'd started flying."

"So what happened?" I asked again. Brad's burger had come, but he ignored it.

"It's kind of hard to say. It passed in a blur. Like I said, I've got a good feeling, but I just don't know whether to trust it or not."

"Trust it," I said, leaning over to plant a kiss on his cheek. "I'm so pleased for you! I'm so proud of you."

He held a hand up. "I'm not there yet, Jo. The next stage is an interview with a pilot and someone from personnel. I might not get there."

"I think you will."

"I hope so. I just can't believe it yet. If I get through – *if* – the training course proper starts in October. In eighteen months, I could be flying a jet!"

I leaned over and kissed him again; this time he held my neck and we kissed properly, on the mouth. When he let me go, I blushed, because the people at the other tables were looking at us.

"Y'see, I've wanted this for ever," he said. "I've wanted to be a pilot since I first saw a plane. Now that I've got a real chance, it's a weird feeling. I feel that I'm within grasp of it at last, but on the other hand, I've still got a long way to go. I could flunk the next stage. I might even have flunked this stage. I'm almost afraid to hope, y'know?"

I put my hand over his and felt the tension in it. "Well then, let me hope for you."

Brad began to eat. The burger had cooled and the cheese was congealing. As he ate, I picked diffidently at the salady bits. Deep inside, my stomach was yawning.

"Have a chip," he said, holding up a glistening golden chunk of potato.

"It's cold," I said.

"No, it isn't. The ones on top are, but the ones underneath aren't."

My stomach grumbled and my mouth watered. I opened my lips and he slipped it inside. The taste was incredible, all crunchy and soft underneath. When I finished it, he fed me another, and then another one.

I was so hungry, I ate the lot. Right at that moment, I wasn't thinking of the fat or the future, I was just happy to be with him, to bask in the elation that radiated from him in waves.

When the chips were gone, Brad pushed the half-eaten burger aside. "I'm just too excited to eat," he said.

I nodded. "I'm so glad for you. I knew you'd do it."

He put his hand on mine and squeezed. "If I did, it's because of you, Jo. You helped. You really did."

I shook my head.

"You did," he insisted. "If you hadn't talked to me about it, I'd've been much more nervous than I was. You listened to me. That made all the difference, Jo."

I gulped, so dizzy that I couldn't reply, couldn't begin to deny it. I felt so guilty, because Mum could've helped him so much more. I decided there and then that I'd introduce him at home before he did the interviews.

We walked home and then we stood outside my house for ages, just gazing at each other.

He kissed me, and then he said he'd ring tomorrow.

"I'm crazy about you, Jo," he said. "I really am."

Indoors, I went upstairs and flopped dreamily on to my bed. For a long time, I thought about Brad and how I felt.

Then I remembered my weight and I thought about the chips. I couldn't remember exactly how many I'd eaten, but it must have been about a hundred grams at least. That's about five hundred calories, although the low-fat oven chips are a bit less.

As I thought about it, the chips formed a hard ball in my stomach. I felt uncomfortably full, uncomfortably fat.

I padded slowly through to the bathroom, where I weighed myself. The digital scale settled on six stones twelve pounds, although it would be more tomorrow, once the chips I'd eaten had turned to fat.

I didn't want to have to make myself sick again, but if I didn't, it would be weeks before I lost the weight I'd just put on. I checked that nobody was in the corridor outside, then I knelt down by the toilet bowl and stuck my fingers down my throat.

I gagged; my throat hurt but nothing came up, so I made myself a huge glass of liver salts, which I gulped down. It tasted vile, but when I stuffed my fingers down my throat a moment later, it did the trick.

I was sick twice. Afterwards, before I pulled the flush, I stared at the clumps of half digested chips floating in the water, with strings of phlegm and froth from the liver salts. I felt awful, as if I'd swallowed a fishing hook and then pulled my stomach inside out. The pain there was sharp and everything else in my body just ached.

I flushed the toilet and then, shakily, I stood up and washed my face. I no longer brushed my teeth with toothpaste because of the calories, but I brushed them with water until my mouth hurt.

There are calories everywhere, even in things where you wouldn't expect them to be, like cough syrup. I'd taken some once to ease my aching throat after I'd been sick, and I'd been horrified to find that the major constituent was syrup. I'd had to make myself sick all over again. The spoonful I'd taken was virtually pure sugar – a hundred and fifty calories at least.

Once I'd finished washing, I put the can of liver salts back. *As a pleasing drink, an aid to digestion, or a laxative*, the label said. *To use as a laxative, take two spoonfuls in a glass of water.*

I'd never thought of using a laxative before, but I took four spoonfuls, just to make sure. I'd rather have diarrhoea than have to force myself to be sick.

Maddie was outside the door when I came out. "Are you OK, Jo? I heard you being sick."

I jumped. "I'm fine, Madds. I just ate a burger and it came back on me."

She looked hard at me. "Sure?"

"Sure. I don't think it was cooked properly."

I felt her eyes follow me as I walked back to my bedroom. I closed the door behind me and sighed with relief.

I'd have to be more careful in future. I didn't want Maddie getting on to my case as well as Brad.

Chapter 10

Brad phoned at half-past eight on Saturday morning; we were supposed to meet up at lunchtime as usual but the hospital had asked him to do overtime. "We could meet up in about ten minutes for breakfast if you like."

"I've only just got out of bed," I mumbled. I was on the phone in the hall and I could sense Dad was listening.

"Oh." His voice sounded sad. "I'm flying tomorrow, so I'll see you Monday," he went on. "I'd ask you to come, 'cept my lesson's at seven a.m., and then I promised to change the oil in Mum's car. I'm working later, of course."

"That's OK," I said. "I'll see you Monday."

"I'll miss you," he said.

I smiled. "Me too."

When I put the phone down, Dad's head popped round the door of his study. "That was Brad, wasn't it? You'll have to bring him round for dinner soon, Jo."

"Yeah," I said. I really would have to if Mum was going to help him get through the interviews.

"We're having the barbecue next Sunday," Dad said. "Why don't you bring him then?"

I frowned. It was one of the Gibson summer rituals to have a barbecue party. It was mainly for the people in Dad's firm, but some of the neighbours came along as well. There's something about the smell of barbecued food that makes my stomach feel like a hungry piranha.

"Maybe," I said, "but he's working at the hospital. He's really busy what with that and his flying lessons."

"I'd like to meet him sometime soon."

"No problem," I said.

At Breeze on Monday morning, I was hanging around with the girls, when Lallie looked out of the window. "Who's that guy?" she asked.

I looked up. It was Brad, and he was waving a letter at me.

I went outside and he lifted me in a bear hug, swinging me right round in a circle before he let me go again.

Then he pushed the letter into my hands. It was from BA, asking him to go for an interview.

"Oh Brad!" I was thrilled for him, I really was.

"It's a bitch about the date," he said.

"Why?"

"Jo! That's when we're supposed to be in Spain! I know it's a pain, but if I get the job, I'll be able to take you anywhere in the world. I get cheap tickets, y'see, so I'll take you to Barbados, Bali – anywhere."

Relief surged through me. I'd been afraid of Spain, because it meant being with him twenty-four hours a day. It meant that I'd have to eat with him, and also, maybe, that I'd sleep with him. At least we'd have the chance to be alone together; I would have been looking forward to it if it hadn't been for that lingering fat.

I wanted so much to look good, look slim. Despite everything that Brad had said, I just knew he'd be turned off if he saw my raw flab.

"I'm really, really sorry," he said.

"That's OK."

"You're not mad with me?"

"Brad, how could I ever be mad with you? I'm just a little sad, that's all." Another lie, but by then I'd already told him quite a few. My mother says that lies destroy a relationship, because they eat away at the trust at the core of it.

"So I'll see you later? I've got to start at four, but I'll take you for a carrot juice if you like."

Since I'd told him I was virtually vegetarian, he'd started to tease me about it.

"OK," I said.

He kissed me on the cheek, and then he left.

When I went back inside, Lallie mock-swooned. "Where've you been hiding him, Jo?" she teased. "He's absolutely gorgeous."

I laughed. "He's too young for you, Lallie."

"Who cares about age? Seriously, he's dreamy, Jo."

"Isn't he just!" Carin said. "I'm jealous, Jo, I really am!"

I felt all warm inside, I couldn't believe that women like that actually fancied my Brad. I smiled to myself, and then I glanced at Naomi. Her face had taken on a mask as hard as stone; her normally pretty features were ugly. There was a very hard look in her eyes. If looks could kill, hers would have done. I think she'd've been happy if I'd just dropped dead.

I was shocked. I hadn't realized how jealous she was.

After a moment, her face softened. As she turned to go to the loo, she patted my stomach playfully. "You've just got to lose that flab, Jo," she said.

The horror that she'd noticed it drove all other thoughts from my mind.

I spent most of that day in the changing rooms. Every spare moment, I sneaked in there to study myself in the mirror. Although the scales that I consulted twice daily told me my weight was heading for six and a half stones, I still looked fat.

I still was fat.

I was in such despair that my life felt like a black hole of hopelessness. Despite all the worry, all the deprivation, the forced vomiting and the laxatives,

I had not lost my flab. I was so desperate that everything else in my life seemed meaningless, even Brad. My feelings for him didn't matter compared to my burning need to be thin.

At lunchtime, I went into Boots and bought two cans of Liver Salts. I decided to take a big dose three times a day.

Just after lunch, Simon appeared. I hadn't seen him since he'd given me the job. Although I'd thought about him, I hadn't missed him at all.

There was something about his presence that made me feel more on edge than I was already. He has this feral, predatory aura that made my skin prickle when he was around. I sensed that the other girls felt it too, because suddenly the tension in the shop was palpable. Simon's eyes were hooded and shaded anyway by the longish dark hair that hung over his brow. He studied us one by one without speaking, as if we were all there for his visual delight.

In a way we were; he owned the place, after all.

"Well, hello!" he said, when his eyes shifted to me. "How are you, darling?"

My throat was dry. "F – fine," I mumbled.

He had a large clothes carrier with him which he hung on the rail and then unzipped. Inside, there were half a dozen glossy party dresses.

"For autumn," he said, taking one gossamer sheath out. "Don't you think this is just divine?"

The dress was made of a very fine luminous fabric that glittered in the light. Although he was speaking to us all, I felt he was addressing me.

"It's very nice," I said slowly. I was wondering how anyone could ever wear a dress like that, because not only would it cling everywhere, it was also almost completely transparent. It was the kind of thing that Hollywood starlets wear when they want to get their picture in the tabloids.

"Only nice?" he asked quizzically, as a look of annoyance shaded his craggy features.

"Well," I said, fumbling for words, "it's the kind of dress that you need to see on."

"Ah," he said slowly, "I know what you mean. Why don't you try it on, Jane?" He was looking at me; there wasn't a Jane in the shop. I was confused for a moment before I realized that he had forgotten my name.

"Jo," I said.

He smiled. "Jo. Go and try it on, Jo, so that we can see what it looks like." He handed the hanger to me. The dress fluttered like a butterfly in the flow of the air conditioning.

"I . . . er . . . it's not the sort of thing I usually wear," I said. "I don't have the right shoes or anything." I looked around desperately. "Naomi has a much better figure than I have."

"But you're so tall, Jo; you're the right height for it. You don't need shoes. Go on, darling, do it for me."

The skin of my face burning, I headed for the changing room. I hung the dress up and stared at

121

it for a moment, then I took my clothes off and put it on.

Simon was right. There was something magical about it, but it was so sheer, so diaphanous, that it made me quake. You could see everything; the outline of my knickers, the little metal widgets on the straps of my bra, even the suggestion of nipples through its cups.

I would wear it – yes, maybe – but only in private, on the first night of my honeymoon if I ever got there. I wondered what Brad would say if he saw me and I trembled inside.

Simon's voice sounded from the door of the changing rooms. "Come on, darling, I'm waiting for you."

I took a deep breath. I could take off the dress there and then. I could leave, just walk out. I hadn't had my wages that week but I could manage without them, and also Dad would pursue Simon all the way to the Antarctic if I told him what had been done to me.

But I didn't. For some reason, I walked out very slowly like I was in a trance, which I was in a way. Simon had this power over me that meant that I couldn't say no to him. I didn't realize it at the time, though. I didn't realize it until much later, when it was too late to change anything.

Like a wraith, I walked out into the shop, where I twirled slowly like a marionette.

None of the girls said anything.

"It's very nice," Simon said, "but, darling, you're wearing too much underwear."

I froze as Naomi sniggered.

Simon didn't touch me, didn't even stand near me, but his gaze made me feel as if I had nothing on at all.

I caught a glimpse of my reflection in the mirrors that surrounded the shop; this girl was slim, attractive, even beautiful. Surely, I thought, it was some trick! That girl wasn't me!

"You could be a model, d'you know that?" Simon said thoughtfully.

I mumbled something, I can't remember what. I was thinking of those Paris fashion shows, with supermodels' boobs hanging out all over the place.

"You must model for me when I do my autumn shows," he said.

I nodded, then I went back to the changing room. Once I was in my clothes again, my senses returned. I was absolutely appalled at what I'd done. My face burned with shame. I stood there while tears formed in my eyes and leaked down my cheeks. The illusion of beauty was gone now; only the fat girl looked back at me.

After a while, Carin came in. I flinched, because I expected her to be angry with me. Simon had made it so clear that it was me he was studying, as well as the dress.

But she wasn't. She hugged me when she saw my tears.

"Don't let him get to you, Jo," she said.

I looked at her. "Why does he do things like that?"

"I don't know. He's a control freak, I guess. I don't think he wants a proper relationship. He just wants to know that you're under his thumb."

"Thanks," I said, drying my tears with the hankie she gave me.

When I met Brad at lunchtime, I didn't say a word about what had happened to me, but he noticed that I was upset.

"What is it?" he asked.

I shook my head. "Nothing. Just a headache, that's all."

"You look kind of peaky."

"It's the air-conditioning in the shop. It makes the air so dry, my throat hurts."

He bought me a big glass of orange juice. Afterwards, to compensate, I took an extra dose of laxative.

In the end I didn't ask Brad to our barbecue; he was working that day. I spent all Saturday making cakes and things, I made a brownie gâteau and two different cheese cakes, banoffee pie and tiramisu.

When I told Dad that Brad couldn't come, he just grunted and said that he still wanted to meet him sometime soon. In a few weeks my parents were going off on their holiday, leaving me and Maddie alone, and I think Dad wanted to have a talk with

Brad to make sure that we wouldn't misbehave while he and Mum were away.

I cringed inside at the thought of it. Surely he knew that with a body like mine, I wouldn't even dream of letting anyone else have a look at it?

The day dawned bright and clear and crisp, with the promise of heat and sunshine later. As Dad lit the barbecue, he and Mum discussed our swimming-pool; we hadn't got one yet but they'd been talking about having one put in for years.

Maddie and I laid out plates and cutlery and glasses. The white wine was chilling in the bath and we'd made gallons of banana daiquiris. The barbecue itself was massive; there was chicken and steaks and king prawns and corn cobs; bowls of salads and quiches as well.

It was agony just to look at it. I know it sounds over the top, but because Dad invites the people who work for him, he writes the whole thing off as a business expense.

When they started to arrive, I busied myself cooking. Maddie was waitressing; as she went past with yet another tray of spritzers, she hissed that she was going to tell Dad that we had to be paid for it.

I laughed as I began to serve the food. Feeding other people always made me feel good.

After a while, everybody had eaten and I was standing alone at the barbecue, contemplating a grizzled steak.

Mum came over. "Go and get something to eat," she said.

"I'm not hungry. I've been snacking the whole day."

"Jo! I've been watching you. You haven't eaten a thing!" She went and got a plate, which she filled with quiche and potato salad and bean salad, all the truly fattening stuff. Then she added a whole garlic baguette.

My stomach yawned like the shark in *Jaws*.

"Eat!" she demanded. "I know you're watching what you eat, Jo, but you're still growing. You've got to get plenty of carbohydrates, or else you'll have no energy at all."

I sat down numbly, terrified that she'd find me out. I began to eat slowly, because there was no way out, but in a moment, I was stuffing myself. Mum watched like a mother hen; when I'd finished, she brought me some brownie gâteau with ice-cream.

"I thought it was all finished," I protested.

"I saved some for you and Maddie. It's only fair, since you two have done all the work."

She watched me for a moment longer and then somebody came to talk to her.

It was too late. I'd already eaten all the gâteau. For a brief moment, I was in heaven. And then the thought of the food began to haunt me, all the things I'd eaten twisted in my mind like angry snakes, each one with a sign that said five hundred calories.

The snakes danced and I groaned, then I got up and went to the bathroom. At first I thought a laxative would be enough, but then I knew I had to make myself sick as well.

With all the calories I'd just eaten, I just knew that my body would be wracked by flab for ever once it got into my blood. I'd eaten three thousand calories or more and I was absolutely certain that every single one of them would turn straight into flab. (By then, I'd completely forgotten that you need to eat in order to survive; that, even if you do nothing at all, your body needs at least fifteen hundred calories a day just to keep ticking over.)

I gulped liver salts until I retched and then I collapsed, too weak even to flush the loo. After a while, my strength returned and I managed to flush it away, then I washed my face.

Maddie was waiting just outside. I hadn't realized it before, but I had forgotten to lock the door.

"I saw that, Jo," she said. "I know what you're doing. You've got to stop."

I leaned back against the wall as a wave of dizziness swept over me.

"It's nothing. It was the fat in the garlic bread, that's all."

Maddie shook her head. "Was it the fat the other night, Jo? You were sick then too, remember? And how many cans of Andrews have you got through this week?"

"Not even one!" I snapped. "Leave me alone,

Maddie. I'm feeling lousy." My anger gave me the strength to walk to my room, but she followed me.

"What's this then?" She was holding up two empty cans which she'd taken from the bathroom bin.

"I've had a stomach upset, that's all. Please, Maddie, stop pestering me."

"Don't lie to me, Jo." She sat down on my bed next to me. "You're hardly eating anything at all, and when you do, you make yourself sick afterwards."

I frowned. "I'm just trying to lose a little weight, that's all."

"Lose weight? Have you looked in a mirror, lately? You're stick thin, Jo. Positively skeletal!"

"I'm not," I yelled.

"You are!"

She grabbed my arms and lifted me up, then she dragged me in front of the mirror. "Look at yourself!"

I did. Although I was wearing a baggy T-shirt, layers of fat lurked underneath it. I could see them despite the clothes. I *knew*, for heaven's sake! It was my body, not hers.

"You try to hide it, but you can't hide it for ever," Maddie said. "You've got to do something before you really hurt yourself, Jo. If Mum and Dad found out what you're doing, they'd have a fit."

Something twanged inside me; it was the beginnings of panic, a terror more acute than anything I'd known before. If Maddie talked to Mum, then

I'd really be in trouble. But Maddie and I never told on each other when we were little; surely she wouldn't now?

"You're not going to tell them?" I whimpered.

"I don't know what to do," she said slowly. "I'm worried that this dieting is going too far. I should've realized it way back, when you got into those size eight jeans."

"Please don't," I moaned. "We don't tell tales, you know that."

"You're making yourself ill, Jo. You've got to stop."

"Please, Maddie," I pleaded, "I'm not going to make myself ill. It's just that I want to get rid of my flab. All the girls at Breeze have brilliant bodies. I feel so gross beside them."

She folded her arms. "That's just it, Jo. You're a waif, you're not gross at all."

I stood very still, listening to the thudding of my racing heart, trying not to give way to the terror inside. I had to do something, I *had* to! If Maddie talked to Mum, that would be the end. I fought the panic for a moment and then a devilish inspiration came. I stepped forward and squinted at the mirror. "You really think so?" I asked, pretending naïvety.

"You're not gross at all," she repeated.

I peered even closer.

"I mean, Jo, for heaven's sake. . ."

"Maybe you're right," I bluffed, closing my mind to what I really saw.

"You're thin, Jo; you really are. I don't think you've got any more fat to lose."

I faked a smile. "Tell me the truth, Madds. D'you really think I can give up my diet?"

She grinned. "Yes, Jo. I'm sure you can."

"Thank goodness," I said. "I was getting really worried. I've been so hungry, I was worried I'd have to starve myself for ever."

"So that's it?" she said hopefully. "No more dieting?"

"I'm not going to guzzle," I said, "but it'll be nice to be able to eat real food again."

She hugged me and then she left.

I sat down on my bed for a moment, until my heart stopped racing. Then I stood up in front of the mirror again.

The same old fat Jo stared back at me, the same Michelin girl with the rolls of fat at the tummy and hips, the same, sturdy tree-trunk thighs.

Maddie didn't know, she couldn't see. She was all tied up with Christian and her course; she didn't know what I was going through. She was wrong. It was just because she'd noticed me being sick, seen the cans of liver salts.

I'd have to be more careful in future. I'd bought myself some time, but if Maddie caught me again, it wouldn't be so easy to talk her out of it.

Chapter 11

Maddie wasn't completely fooled; she began to watch me after that. At breakfast, she watched me eat All-Bran, and at night, she watched as I ploughed through a baked potato and cheese and tons of vegetables. Afterwards, for supper she'd make me cocoa and toast with butter *and* honey. I couldn't do anything about it, because she watched the loo as well. It was as if I had an albatross at my shoulder, but she wasn't an albatross, she was my sister.

If I went out, she'd say, "I'll come with you". I couldn't say "no", else she might tell them.

I think she even searched my room for liver salts.

If she wasn't my sister, I would have started to hate her.

In fact, I hated her anyway, even though she was my sister.

By the time I got to work it was too late to make

myself sick, so I just took a triple dose of liver salts. I was doing that one day when Lallie saw me.

"De toxing?" she asked. She's a fitness freak, always exercising and fretting about vitamins and wholefoods.

"Mmm," I mumbled.

"That stuff's useless," she said. She told me to try this powder that comes in sachets and makes an orange drink. I went and bought some at lunchtime. That night, after dinner, I made myself a big glass which I drank as we watched a re-run of *Pretty Woman*. Maddie had no idea what I was doing. I'd already burned the sachets, so she had no way of finding out.

In fact, she approved of my orange squash. That night, she didn't make cocoa.

Inside, I laughed at her. At the end of the week, I'd put on a couple of pounds. When I showed her that, her scrutiny began to ease a little. I was relieved, although inside I was panicking. I just had to get those extra pounds off again. The fat would kill me if I didn't get rid of it. My battle with my body was becoming a war.

Brad was working every day at the hospital. He was having two flying lessons a week, and kept on asking me if I thought that he was being selfish. The only time we saw each other was at lunch or on weekend mornings; his shift started at three and it didn't finish until eleven o'clock at night.

I assured him that he wasn't being selfish and I

didn't mind that we weren't going out. It was partly because I knew how much his flying meant to him, but mainly because I didn't want to have to eat any more food, which I would if we went out together.

I'd taken to wearing a baggy cardigan when I wasn't at work, not to hide my fat so much as to try to hide the fact that I was trying to lose it.

One lunchtime we were in the coffee bar. It was a Friday and Brad was looking concerned about something. I asked him what.

"Nothing really," he said. "It's just this little girl came in yesterday afternoon. She'd swallowed something noxious so they gave her some stuff to make her sick and then they called me to take her up to the ward. It wasn't quite out of her system and she was sick all over me."

"Yuk!"

"I know." He brushed his hair sheepishly. "I'm still afraid I stink."

My interest quickened. "You don't," I said. "What did they give her to make her sick?"

"Some vile concoction; it's called an emetic. "

"An emetic?"

"Yeah. One gulp makes you sick instantly. Usually they wash stomachs out but they'd given this girl an emetic for some reason. I don't know, she was just a kid. Why d'you ask?"

I fiddled with my glass of mineral water. "No reason. Just interest, that's all." I saw Maddie standing at the sandwich counter and I ducked down, because I didn't want her to see me without food. If she did, she'd nag me about it.

Puzzled, Brad peered at me. "What is it?"

I held my finger to my lips. Ages passed before Maddie paid for her sandwich and left.

"That was my sister," I said.

"Why are you avoiding her?"

"We had a row last night," I fibbed.

He frowned. "What about?"

My mind whirled as I began to invent an elaborate lie.

That afternoon, I asked Carin if I could pop out to the chemists.

"Sure," she said, "but I've got paracetamol and Tampax, if that's what you need."

"I've to pick up a prescription," I said.

There was nothing called an emetic on the shelves so I went to the counter and asked. The woman didn't know; she went and asked the pharmacist.

"What d'you want an emetic for?" he asked, fixing me with a steely gaze.

"Um . . . my mother asked me to get her some."

"Are you sure it was an emetic?" he asked.

I could tell from his expression that he didn't believe me. "I think so," I shrugged.

"We don't sell emetics," he said.

My stomach sank. "Who does?" I asked desperately.

"Nobody," he said. "It's something that's only administered under medical supervision."

"But my mother—"

"You'd better tell her to see her doctor. If you give me your doctor's name, I'll ring for you."

"Uh . . . don't bother." I turned and fled, feeling his suspicious eyes following me. Once I was far enough away, I had to stop to give my heart a chance to return to it's normal rhythm.

Breeze was empty when I got back but then it often is; you don't need many customers when each one spends five hundred pounds or so. I stood there, listening to the music and wondering how I could get my hands on some of that stuff Brad had told me about.

I don't trust laxatives, you see. OK, they flush you out, but only once the food's been right through the digestive system. All the fat and sugar has already been absorbed.

That night I went to the hospital. It was really busy because it was Friday night and there was a load of drunks. I was terrified that Brad would see me, but he must have been somewhere else. I had the luck of the devil that night.

I hung around the nurse's station pretending that I was waiting for someone. After a while, they no longer noticed me. I watched carefully and realised to my dismay that all the drugs and stuff were kept locked away. Only the nurses had the keys.

It was hopeless, but I was desperate. Right then, my life depended on getting the stuff. Just after nine, there was a mad panic when the victims of a car crash were brought in. The drugs cupboard was left open. I slipped in and grabbed a likely looking bottle from the top shelf, then I scuttled away with it dragging in my rucksack. I ran all the way home.

It wasn't the fear of being caught stealing, it was the fear of losing what I'd stolen.

On Saturday morning, Mum and Dad went off to the garden centre and Maddie went with them. For the first time in ages, I was alone in the house.

I gazed at the bottle for a long time. The label was smudged, the name was an inky blur, but below that I could just make out the word: *EMETIC*. I smiled to myself as I twisted the cap off. The liquid inside smelled vile. I drank a little and gagged. A moment later, I was so sick that I couldn't reach the bathroom in time. I spewed all over the carpet and then again and again in the toilet bowl.

I must have vomited for about half an hour. It was continuous; at one point I was afraid that I'd really hurt myself. Afterwards, I was too weak to do anything. I lay on the cold tiled bathroom floor for ages before I found the energy to get up and clean up the mess. My whole digestive system felt like it was on fire.

The emetic had certainly worked. I looked at it again and saw the phrase *use dilute* on the label. I'd taken it straight. I shuddered; I could have made myself really ill.

Next time, I'd know better.

The phone rang. It was Brad. I'd completely forgotten that I was supposed to be meeting him.

"You sound awful," he said, anxiously.

"I'm OK, it's just hayfever," I lied. I could no longer count how many lies I'd told him. "I'm really sorry. I was sneezing all night. I've only just woken up."

"It's all right, I understand," he said. "I've got tomorrow off; I didn't know about it because I didn't look at my shifts until last night. Wanna go down to Brighton? Dad says I can use his new car."

"Haven't you got a flying lesson?"

"Nope. I'd rather spend the time with you anyway."

My fingers tightened around the phone.

"Jo, are you there?"

"I'm here."

"I'll pick you up tomorrow, about nine?"

"Um . . . OK," I agreed. As I put down the phone, I began to think up excuses so that I wouldn't have to eat.

By that stage, I truly hated my body. It had betrayed me, you see; it would not obey me. No matter how hard I dieted, how many laxatives I took, how many times I vomited, I still couldn't get rid of the fat. It clung to me like a vampire bat and made me hate myself.

Every waking moment was taken up with the need to get rid of it. I spent hours staring at myself in the mirror, even longer gazing at the bathroom

137

scales. Although the scales told me that I was hovering around six and a half stones, I was pretty sure that Maddie had tampered with them so that they gave a false result.

The scales told me that I should be thin, but the mirror told me that I was still fat. The waist of my size eight jeans now seemed a little loose, but I doubted that too. Maddie's so devious, I thought maybe she'd swapped them for a larger pair and switched the size tag when my back was turned.

The way she watched me so intently was making me paranoid. When I dressed to meet Brad the next day, I wore a floaty top on top of my jeans, and a baggy sweatshirt on top of that. My body was so horrible that I couldn't bear anyone to look at it.

"Hiya!" he said, as I got into the car. He leaned over to kiss me. I was really nervous, but he didn't seem to notice. On the way to Brighton, we talked about the next stage of pilot selection; he was worried about the interviews. I tried to calm him as best I could, but I knew it would be much better if he came to talk to Mum.

I wasn't looking forward to that. In fact, the prospect terrified me. The A levels results were due soon, and a dark little voice inside me said that if Brad didn't get the grades he needed, the problem would go away.

When we got to Brighton, we walked along the pebbled beach for a while, and then we went to the pier, where Brad played computer games and

I watched. The sky was cloudless, but a strong sea breeze made it just a shade chilly, so I didn't look unusual in my thick sweatshirt.

The game was something about defending a princess against aliens; Brad's score was so high that he won a free go, but he turned away from the console and took my hand.

"It's not fair, you should play too," he said.

I shrugged. "I enjoy watching." Just then the machine bleeped hollowly and a message on the screen told him he'd lost the chance of a free game. Another one would cost him 50p.

"That's it," he laughed. "Thing is," he said, "these computer games are a bit like flying a big commercial jet. Your reactions have to be spot on, and you've got to focus on the main task, despite all the distractions. You have to analyse lots of different bits of information simultaneously."

"Hmm," I said. "I don't think I could do that." I hadn't forgotten the excitement I'd felt when that instructor offered me a cheap flying lesson, but I knew that I'd never have the courage to try. I mean, I couldn't even lose my fat, so how could I ever fly a plane myself?

"Sure you could," Brad said, turning back to the machine, where he put another 50p in and handed the controls to me.

I panicked. I don't know why, but I've never been interested in computer games; they just don't appeal to me. About twenty different things happened at once and the poor princess hardly had a taste of freedom before she ended up in the clutches of a monster.

"You see," I said to Brad.

"Rats, Jo! You always crash first time. Wanna try again?"

"No. I've never played computer games before. I'm too old to start now."

"Gee, Jo," he teased me, "I didn't know you'd been so deprived." He put his hands in his pockets. "I've got some on the PC at home. Dad used to play them all the time when he was out of work. He said the distraction kept him sane."

"I'd be afraid I'd get addicted."

"It can be addictive, I s'pose. They're fiendishly clever, most of them. It's so real, you get totally involved. Lucy got me this brilliant one at Christmas. It's a flight simulator. It's got diagrams of various airports and you have to land a jet. It's pretty easy, but there's all these different levels, weather conditions, holding patterns and so on. You can make it quite difficult. I played it all the time. I feel really guilty about it now."

"Why?"

"I didn't want to cheat when I did the BA aptitude tests, but I know Hong Kong airport like the back of my hand, JFK too. I mean, a monkey could probably pass if it'd practised on that computer programme."

I felt a rush of love for him then. That was my Brad: so straight, so true, so *honest*. It made me feel all warm and gooey until I remembered all the lies I'd told him.

If only I could lose that fat, I could love him properly! I wouldn't be ashamed of my body, I'd be able to be with him, to eat with him, and enjoy it. I wouldn't be constantly on edge in case he noticed my fat, or worried about my diet. OK, it's sad about his sister, but I'm not like that. There's a difference between wanting to lose weight and becoming anorexic.

"Brad," I said, "everybody else who's applied for pilot training has probably played that game to death. It shows initiative, that's all."

He grinned as he took my hand. "I confessed anyway," he said. "There was a question about computer games. I said I'd got a flight simulator."

We walked along the front and then into The Lanes, a quaint olde worlde tangle of shops and restaurants.

Brad stopped at an Indian place. Before my diet, I used to adore Indian food; Tandoori was my favourite, closely followed by Chicken Tikka Masala. The first time Brad and I ever ate together was at the Indian restaurant in town.

"Hungry?"

"Er . . . not yet. Dad always cooks breakfast on Sundays. I must've had a pound of bacon."

He squinted at me. "I thought you'd gone vege-tarian."

I turned away and peered at the menu in the window. "It's far too expensive, Brad. Aren't you meant to be saving up for flying lessons?"

He sighed.

"I'm not hungry, I'm really not," I said again. "I had a huge breakfast."

"Jo, it's after three o'clock. Besides, it looks really good. I made over two hundred quid last week, so I can afford it."

He pushed the door open. I followed, trying not to inhale the scent of fresh coriander and chilli and Tandoori.

The place was half empty so we got a table immediately. The waiter brought iced water and, without us asking, a pile of poppadoms. My mouth watered and my stomach cried out.

Brad broke off a bit for himself, another which he fed to me. I ate, trying to ignore the taste. I was thinking. I had no laxatives with me and my precious emetic was at home; by the time I got there, it would be too late.

I didn't look at the poppadoms again, but then I didn't need too; Brad was so hungry that he wolfed the lot. When the waiter came, he ordered some more. "What d'you want?" he asked me.

"Um. . ." I stared at the menu, searching for something that was fat free.

Brad and the waiter waited for a while, but I took so long that in the end Brad ordered for me: Butterfly prawns, then Chicken Tikka Masala with Naan bread and Onion Bhajis.

"I know you like that," he said, as the waiter left. "No red meat."

"I'd rather you let me order myself," I said, churlishly.

He looked hurt. We waited in silence for the food to come.

The Butterfly prawns came in a single dish and Brad divided them between our plates. As he ate, I toyed with one, telling myself that it wasn't delicious, that my taste-buds were deceiving me. I was in agony; I wanted desperately to eat, but I couldn't risk it because Brad would notice if I made myself sick.

There was a commotion as a waiter dropped a plate, and when Brad turned to look I quickly put all but one of my prawns on his plate. There were several there and so I hoped he wouldn't notice, and when he turned back to his food, he didn't seem to.

So I got away with eating just one and a half butterfly prawns; I mashed the other half into oblivion and hid it underneath my fork.

Then came the Chicken Tikka Masala, a fragrant mass of spices and cream, sizzling and glistening with calories and fat.

Again, Brad served both of us. I ate a little rice, but I just couldn't bear to touch the chicken. It was too rich. The longer I didn't touch it, the more pleased I was with myself. I really must have some self control after all, I thought, if I could manage not to eat a plateful of a food that I really adored.

Then Brad asked me why I wasn't eating anything.

"I told you, I'm not very hungry," I said.

"I picked you up at half-past nine, it's at least six hours since you've eaten."

"I had a big breakfast. I'm just not hungry. It's not a crime."

"Jo, you love Chicken Tikka Masala."

"I've changed my mind. How dare you tell me what I like!" Anger was beginning to throb inside me. "It's full of fat. I just don't want to clog all my blood vessels up."

Brad put his fork down and took a drink of water. "I saw you putting your prawns on my plate."

"I didn't want to waste them, that's all."

"Why didn't you just ask me if I wanted them?"

"Because I knew you'd make a fuss, just like you're doing now. Stop pestering me, Brad. It's not a big deal, it really isn't."

"Jo." He put his hands on the table; he looked at them and then at me. "You're still dieting, aren't you?"

I shook my head vigorously. "I'm just careful what I eat, that's all."

"Jo," he said again. His voice was pleading. "I've been through this before, remember? I've seen it all before."

"What have you seen before?" I demanded.

"My sister nearly starved herself to death, Jo. I didn't see all of it, but I saw enough."

My heart was beating like a thunderclap. "Don't be ridiculous, Brad."

"I'm not being ridiculous, Jo. I watched Lucy. I

saw her doing all these things. I watched her put food on my plate when she thought I wasn't looking. I watched the way she looked at the food on her plate, as if it would attack her. I saw the fear in her eyes. I saw the way her hair went all stringy and thin, like yours is. I saw her skin all pale and clammy, just like yours."

"You're being absurd," I said.

"Jo, please don't do this to me."

"I'm not doing anything to you, Brad. I just watch my weight, that's all. It's not a crime, and it's not an illness either. For God's sake, a third of the women in this country do the same thing!"

"Jo, *please*! Please don't do this to me. Please. I couldn't bear it if it happened to you too."

"Nothing's going to happen to me," I snapped.

He reached for my hand, but I tugged it away. "I saw Lucy, Jo. She used to be just the way you are now."

"That's ridiculous!"

"Jo, please listen to me. You've got to get help before it gets any worse."

"*How dare you tell me what to do!*" I roared. A sudden silence came over the restaurant; my face burned as I realized that the other diners were staring at us.

Brad leaned closer. "I mean it, Jo. I wouldn't say it if I didn't care, if I didn't know. But I do. You have to do something before it's too late."

"I don't need you or anybody else to tell me what to do!" I snarled. "How dare you! *How dare you!*"

"Because I care about you," he said, very simply.

I got up and stormed out of the restaurant. He rose to follow me but the waiter came running with the bill.

"Please don't do this to me, Jo."

I couldn't bear to be with him any more. When I got outside, I ran to the station. I had no idea a ticket home cost so much; it was more money than I had so I had to pay with Dad's credit card.

I'd have to explain it when I got home, but I knew I'd rather do that than argue with Brad.

On the journey home, I began to cry.

I could hardly bear the thought of losing Brad, but then I couldn't keep him either, not when he was nagging me the way he had. What Naomi said about some boys not wanting their girlfriends to be too attractive flashed through my mind, but it wasn't that. It was just him panicking because his sister had had anorexia. It was crazy really, because if he saw how fat I was, he'd go off me anyway.

I thought about it all the way home. Without him, I could diet properly, I'd have a real chance to lose my fat.

Afterwards, I would go back to him, ask that we give it another chance. He needed some time to get over that silly idea that I was crazy, like his sister had been.

And I would be thin then.

The train wheel clattered rhythmically. *Ta ta ta,*

tattata ta! Just like the mantra that wound around my head:

He *will* love me when I'm thin. Everything will be perfect then.

Chapter 12

When I got home, I told Dad that we'd fallen out. He asked some questions, but I didn't answer them. I went and lay in my room. When the phone rang a while later, I heard him answer it.

It was Brad. Dad raved on at him for daring to leave his daughter stranded and then he banged the phone down.

I smiled briefly; I was still angry with Brad but then I began to worry if I really would be able to get him back.

I stared at my face in the mirror. My hair had always been thin, but it wasn't stringy. And my skin was naturally pale. I didn't *think* I looked so bad, but I also didn't know if I could trust the mirror any more.

I was split in two. On one side there was Brad, on the other there was my body. I'd never be able to keep him if I was fat, but then maybe I couldn't keep him anyway. Maybe I didn't deserve someone like that.

If only I could be thin! If only I didn't have to worry about the way I looked! He said he wanted me to eat, but if I ate I'd be fat, and then he'd hate me anyway.

The days passed and although I was really sad about Brad, I was relieved that I could get on with my diet. As time passed, I convinced myself that it was all because of my body, that as soon as I was really thin, as soon as I had got rid of that pernicious fat, everything would be fine again. Now Maddie was the only one I had to worry about. When she was around I had to eat, but I tried to make sure it was vegetables, not carbohydrate. Because I was cooking our meals, it was easy to mislead her. I kept on with the laxatives, but I saved my emetic for emergencies.

I didn't tell Naomi about Brad, but after a few days she asked me why I hadn't mentioned him for a while.

"Umm. . ." I mumbled.

"Did he chuck you?"

"No. We had a row."

"Is that the end, then?" There was a glimmer in her eye.

"I don't know. I just needed some space, that's all." I knew that Naomi hated me because of Brad. I didn't know what had happened with her guy in Cornwall since her mother found out she went to see him that weekend, and I wasn't going to ask because I didn't want to be bitchy.

But Naomi kept on making bitchy comments about my weight. I wished that I could ignore her, but I just couldn't.

It wasn't the end of our friendship that bothered me; I didn't care about that. All I cared about at that time was my desperate need to lose my fat, and Naomi knew that.

Lallie had a perfect body. I asked her one day how she managed to keep it like that.

Lallie sighed. "It's a constant struggle," she said. "I eat mainly vegetables and fruit, only a little protein. I can't touch carbohydrates, because they get me right here." She patted her thighs. "I work out three times a week and the other days I power walk for four miles."

"Sounds tough," I said.

"It is. It's what you've got to do if you want a perfect body."

"Lallie. . ." I began. I was going to ask her what she thought of my body, but my courage faltered.

She smiled at me. "That's why I envy you young girls so much. The teenage metabolism just burns fat up. You don't have to struggle the way you have to do when you're in your twenties."

I gaped at her as she left. If only she knew how I had to struggle too!

I'd almost stopped thinking of the real Brad. He'd become a mythical character in my mind, who'd arrive on a white stallion once I was thin and carry me off to a life of bliss. In my dreams, he was there, but not in reality; I was living in a fantasy world most of the time, so his physical absence didn't bother me too much, or so I told myself.

I bumped into him one day when I was going to work. I was so surprised, because I'd been walking along thinking about him. It wasn't until later that I realized he'd been waiting for me.

"How's things?" he asked.

I was shivering inside, terribly afraid that he could read my thoughts, where we'd been sunbathing on a beach in the Caribbean. Of course, in my dream I had a perfect body, even though only moments before the mirror had told me that I was still absolutely gross.

"OK," I replied, a shade too sharply. "And you?"

"OK." He pushed his hands into his pockets. "My interview's next week."

"I hope you do well. I think you will."

"Maybe. I got my A level results last week. I got three Bs, so that's a start."

"Mmm." I'd sneaked a look at the results on the school noticeboard, so I already knew what he'd got, but I didn't want him to know that.

"I was going to phone you sometime."

"Phone me and tell me how you get on," I said.

"OK. I'm not exactly your dad's favourite person."

"They'll be on holiday by then." We'd nearly reached Breeze; I kept on walking.

He stopped. "Take care," he said.

"You too."

I walked into Breeze, unable to believe that I'd left him standing there, just like that.

Mum and Dad were leaving on Friday. On Wednesday night, Maddie came into my room. She had a large envelope in her hand. Although she'd said nothing about my diet since the barbecue, things were pretty strained between us. I hated the way she watched over me eat.

By then, the size eight jeans were inside my wardrobe, along with the other size eight clothes I'd bought and the large M had long since been consigned to the waste-bin. It never had done me any good.

"I'm still worried about you, Jo," she began.

"Maddie!" I interrupted, exasperated. "For heaven's sake, I'm eating well. You've seen me. I've put on three pounds in the last week alone." That was a lie. According to the scales I was six and a half stones, but I was so sure that they were wrong I told myself that it might be true.

"You're still too thin, Jo. You're sixteen, so you're still growing—"

"I'm nearly seventeen!" I snapped.

"You need energy," Maddie insisted. "You need some flesh, but you're like a rake."

"I am not!"

"You are, Jo. You don't look well, you really

don't. You're always weighing yourself, and you're a bundle of nervous energy. You never stop."

"*Maddie!*"

"I mean it, Jo. Look, I got these leaflets from the Eating Disorders Association."

"The *what*?"

"The Eating Disorders Association. I'm really worried you've got anorexia, Jo. There's a girl at Uni who has it and you're just like her."

She took a leaflet out of the envelope and handed it to me.

I didn't even look at it. "I haven't got anorexia, Maddie."

"Maybe not, but I'm worried that you're heading that way."

"Don't joke."

"Just look at yourself, Jo."

"I *am* looking at myself, Maddie." I stood up and gazed at the mirror. My brain told me that I'd lost some weight, but there was still fat around my waist and my hips. My thighs were, as ever, tree-trunks.

She brushed her hair back. "I don't want to say anything to Mum and Dad. It would ruin their holiday."

My heart-rate soared as she threatened me again. I struggled to pretend that I didn't care. "So don't tell them. I've stopped dieting anyway, so there's nothing to tell. It's all in your head, Maddie, you're imagining things."

"I am not, Jo. You're still way too thin. I don't

think you eat at all, apart from when there's someone watching you."

I turned away so that she wouldn't see the expression on my face. "I'm eating sensibly," I said. "It took an age for the fat to come off, so it'll take a while to come back on again."

Inside, I was cringing at the thought of it.

She gazed at me. "I'm worried that there's something wrong, Jo. You're not normal, you're not the old Jo at all. It might help if you talked to somebody about how you feel."

My mind was whirling, veering between the impulse to deny what she'd said and the need to stop her from telling our parents. I mean, the very idea was ridiculous; it was like this brain virus was going around, making people think that Jo Gibson was too thin! Nevertheless, I couldn't bear to have Mum and Dad on my case as well. I had plans for the time when they'd be away.

"Have you any idea what it would do to me if something happened to you?" she demanded. "What it would do to all of us?"

"Maddie, nothing's going to happen to me."

"Jo, I'm your *sister*! If I didn't care, I wouldn't bother, but I do. I don't want to hurt you, but I don't want you to hurt yourself either, and I'm afraid that you will. I'm afraid you already have. I don't want to talk to Mum and Dad about it, especially if you don't want me to, but if you won't listen to me what else can I do?"

"What d'you want me to do?" I asked her. The

only way out of this was to go along with her. Once Mum and Dad were gone, all her threats would be empty.

"Well, there's a local support group. If you went along to that it'd be a start."

I sat down next to her. "Maddie, I don't have anorexia. I'm not at all like that woman. I'm eating properly. I'm not crazy."

"I'm not saying you are. I'm just saying that your weight means far too much to you. You think you're fat, but you're thin. You're not seeing things as they really are, Jo."

"I just hate myself when I'm fat, Maddie," I cried.

"Will you go to the group, just once, for me? The address is on the leaflet."

I glanced at the leaflet and saw that the next meeting was nearly four weeks away. I gave in. "OK, I'll go. Now will you stop worrying, Maddie?"

"Yeah, Jo. I don't want to worry about you, I really don't. It's just you hear these stories, and I'd hate to hear one that was about you."

After she left I wondered why it was that only I could see myself; everybody else was obviously seeing someone else.

Naomi came round on Sunday morning.

I looked at her quizzically as I opened the door. Maddie was listening to some Gregorian chants on the CD player at full volume. I know, that's almost a contradiction in terms, but that's the way Maddie likes her Gregorian chants. Christian liked early Church music, and so it reminded her of him.

He was phoning her every night and they'd croon sweet nothings into each other's ears right into the small hours.

It was almost as sickening as the emetic, which, incidentally, I'd hidden on the top shelf of the garden shed.

"I've got something to tell you," Naomi said.

I let her in, only because I didn't feel up to a row.

"Jo," she said, once she'd teased the suspense out with small talk about Breeze, "I don't want to tell you this, but I have to."

I waited.

"I saw Brad last night," she said.

I folded my arms. "I thought you were still under a curfew."

"I am, but Mum took me to see the new Spielberg film. As we were coming out, I saw Brad with another girl."

I fiddled with my nails.

"It wasn't his sister," she said. I knew that she was waiting for me to say something, but I decided not to give her the satisfaction.

"Aren't you interested?" she went on.

"Not really. He's pretty much a free agent these days. We both are." I was screaming inside, struggling for a nonchalance that I didn't feel.

"They weren't actually holding hands, but they seemed *very* close."

I was thinking, the cinema complex backs on to the hospital; it might be a nurse, someone he'd met there. It could be just an acquaintance, a casual friend, but then I thought, some hope! Brad's gorgeous, a really nice person too. He was bound to meet someone else.

He probably hadn't even meant it when he'd said he was crazy about me. Maybe he was trying to sugar me up so I'd go to bed with him.

He'd said he didn't want to rush me, but what he'd meant was that he wasn't so keen on the idea of going to bed with someone whose lower body looked like the Michelin Man. I could understand that.

I picked up a skewer and began to stab at my cuticles.

"Are you upset?"

I stared at her. "Why should I be upset? I told you, we had a row."

"You didn't tell me what it was about."

I'd stabbed at the cuticle so hard that the nail-bed had begun to bleed. "It's really none of your business, Naomi. Maddie's having some friends round and I promised to cook lunch. I have to start now."

"I'm sorry," she said, "but I had to tell you. We *are* friends."

"Don't be absurd!" I snapped. "We were only friends so long as it was convenient to you. I don't think you know the meaning of the word."

She stood up. "You've changed, Jo."

I shook my head. "I got real, that's all."

As soon as I'd closed the door behind her, I ran upstairs and cried for hours, with Maddie's Gregorian chants ringing in my ears.

I told myself that I was stupid, that I shouldn't let her get to me like that.

But it didn't help.

She had.

Chapter 13

I gorged myself that day. For the first time in ages, I ate everything I wanted to eat. Deep inside, I hated myself, but Maddie looked pleased. When Christian phoned that evening, I sneaked out to the garden shed, where I took some of the precious liquid. I diluted it with water, but I was violently sick all over Mum's rose beds.

Afterwards, I hated myself even more.

I got through the days somehow, by telling myself that I didn't care about Brad. In a way, I didn't. The only thing that mattered to me was my body and the fat, the rest of my life had come to a halt. Somehow I managed to convince Maddie that I was eating properly, but in actual fact, I wasn't eating at all.

I'd always had bad days – you know, days when life doesn't seem worth living, when everything's bleak, when I felt that I was useless, worthless to myself and everyone else. But at that time, every day was a bad day. I don't know how I managed to keep going, to keep on working at Breeze, but somehow I did.

In the past few months, I'd become so practised at hiding what I was doing that it wasn't so hard to hide what I felt as well.

The sale was on at Breeze and the shop was busy for once; that distracted me. But the main thing was my dreams, my fantasy of how perfect life would be when I managed to get my weight under control properly.

Brad phoned once. A thrill ran through me when I heard his voice, but then I remembered that he'd met someone else.

"How did it go?" I asked him mechanically.

"It hasn't gone yet," he replied. "It's in two days' time. I just phoned to say 'hello', that's all."

"Good luck," I said, dully.

"Jo?"

"Yes?"

"I'm . . . I'm missing you. I'd really like to see you again."

"So w—" My grip tightened on the handset. Why on earth was he playing games with me? "Maybe," I said, "but I'm pretty busy these days."

I hung up without saying "goodbye", and then I cried until I fell asleep.

The next day was my half-day off. I wandered into the mall, my stomach aching. In the department store, there was a display of really expensive hair conditioners. I bought some, ignoring the cost. And some make-up, because, maybe, I was a touch pale.

The saleswoman suggested that I might be anaemic, so I went into Boots and bought some vitamins and iron. I still felt lousy, so I went into another shop, where I bought a couple of long floaty dresses that would hide my flab, and sandals to go with them.

As I passed the department store on my way out of the mall, I saw a jacket in the window that I really liked too, so I bought it as well, and new jeans and a bag to go with it. I'd run out of cash by that stage, so I used Dad's credit card.

At home, I ran a bath which I filled with salts and foam. I soaked for a while and then I changed into one of the new dresses I'd bought. I was still fat. I went for a run but after half a mile my legs cramped so much that I had to give up. I stood there panting, as people stared at me.

I'm sixteen, for God's sake! I thought. Surely, for once in my life, I'll be able to get my body the way I want it to be?

Breeze's sale was over. We were stocking the racks with the new season's lines when Simon appeared. It was just before closing time, and we were all pretty ragged, because we'd been working hard all day.

Simon had a bottle of chilled champagne which he opened to celebrate the end of the sale. Breeze had never taken so much money as it had during the previous week. We all had a glass, although I had just the merest sip of mine, because of the calories.

"Let's go out," he said. Although he was speaking to us all, once again I felt as if he was talking just to me. I looked down at the clothes I was wearing; although it was all designer stuff it was as tired as I was.

He caught my glance. "You look wonderful," he said.

He was staring at me. I couldn't believe that this man was interested in me, but he was! His gaze was as tender as a lover's touch, but there was heat too that smouldered openly in his eyes.

I was entranced. For a moment, it was as if my dreams had come true. Simon wasn't Brad, but he was a man; he wouldn't look at me this way if I was fat. The spell held for a moment longer and then broke as he held the door open and told the others to come along.

Simon took us to this restaurant where I'd never been before, although my parents go there on special occasions. It's on the river and it's very good, but it's outrageously expensive. When we got there, it was still early, so we had the bar to ourselves. Although it was the height of summer, a log fire was burning in the grate and for once the perpetual feeling of cold left me. Simon ordered more champagne, which I sipped slowly as I listened to the others talking to him. Her curfew suspended for dinner with the boss, Naomi was babbling on about the latest Japanese designer, trying to show off the knowledge that she'd gleaned from that month's *Vogue*, but I could sense that Simon was bored. His eyes constantly swept the room; occasionally they met mine.

Carin looked resigned and I remembered what Naomi had told me. I now knew that she lived in a flat that Simon owned, although not with him, and I felt briefly sorry for her.

When other people began to arrive, we went through to the restaurant, where we had a window table. Naomi sat to my right and Lallie to my left. Carin was on Lallie's left so Simon was sitting directly opposite me. As the waiter brought the menus, I distracted myself with a sip of champagne. It fizzled on my tongue and spread a warm, woozy feeling through my stomach.

I floated dreamily, aware that as soon as I looked in a mirror the ugly truth would take over again, but until I did I could imagine that I really was slim.

When Simon asked me what I wanted to eat, I jumped. I hadn't even looked at the menu; I just knew that everything was hopelessly rich and calorific.

"Jo's on a diet," Naomi smirked.

"Shall I order for you?" Simon asked.

I nodded dumbly, and he asked for oysters and then grilled lobster with a salad. There were no prices on our menus, but I knew that oysters and lobsters cost a fortune.

"Please, no," I said. "Just a salad would be fine."

Simon smiled, his teeth radiant white against his sun-tan. "Trust me, Babes. Oysters have hardly any calories at all."

I demurred, thinking vaguely of the word "Babes". It was the kind of name that Maddie would say was demeaning, but it felt strangely alluring when he called me that. I took another sip of champagne and savoured the feeling. I don't normally drink at all, but at home we always have wine with special meals, so I wasn't too worried about it.

The food came. I didn't know what to do with my oysters. Simon picked one up and teased the flesh from the shell, which he fed to me with a fork.

"Hardly any calories," he said, "and it's *so* delicious!"

I swallowed, tasting nothing more than a vague tang of the sea. He fed me another, then another. I was transfixed, unable to refuse. All his attention was on me. Once the oysters were finished, he didn't look away.

The silence was heavy and I felt obliged to fill it. "Why did you start Breeze?" I asked him.

"Because I love women."

The words sent a shiver down my spine. It wasn't that I was falling for him or anything like that, it was the idea that he was falling for me. I mean, he was rich and successful, the stuff of magazine fantasies. I was hurting about Brad so much, I'd've been delighted if a baboon had shown any interest in me.

The lobster came and once again he fed me; my stomach had been empty for so long that all the food made it feel uncomfortably full.

"I adore girls like you," he said. "You just don't know how beautiful you are."

After the plates were cleared away and the waiter brought coffee, he asked me about my plans for the rest of my life.

"Um . . . just to live it, I guess."

"No ambitions, hopes, dreams?"

To be thin, I almost said, but then I said that I wanted to be happy and do some good for the world. Like rid the air of pollutants, stop the desecration of the rain forests, and share food and medicine so that nobody goes hungry any more or dies needlessly.

"You're too altruistic," he said.

"Jo's always been a good girl," Naomi sneered.

"That's OK," he said dismissively, returning to me. Out of the corner of my eye, I saw Carin fidgeting with the clasp of her bag. I wanted to bring her into the conversation, but I was so woozy with champagne that I couldn't think of a way to do that. I was split again, between the part of me that knew what Simon was doing and didn't like it, and the part that said it was the only time that a man like that would pay attention to me, so I'd better enjoy it while he did.

Then he ordered more champagne, and although I had only a couple of sips of mine, I'd had enough to break free of the chains of reality. I began to laugh and joke with him; I was actually flirting, something I'd never dreamed of doing before. I'd never had the confidence.

His mobile phone rang; he took the call then clicked the off button, frowning. "I have to go, darlings," he said. "I'll ask them to get a taxi for you."

I deflated like a burst balloon, but on the way out of the restaurant, he took my arm and said that he would drive me home.

"Do you really have to go?" I asked, as I got into his car. (As I said, I wasn't really behaving like myself at all.)

His face shaded. "Yes. There's a problem at one of my other businesses."

I remembered that Naomi had told me he had a nightclub on the river as well.

He had a Porsche convertible and the top was down. I stretched my legs and inhaled the scent of expensive leather. As we passed the Town Hall, I saw that the time was just after eleven.

"You couldn't go past the hospital, could you?"

He shrugged and made a right turn at the lights. I ran my fingers through my hair, tangled by the wind.

"You're not going out with a doctor, are you?"

I smiled. "No. Nothing like that."

"What then?"

"A mystery. You'll just have to wonder about it, Simon."

As he drove past the entrance to Accident and Emergency, there was Brad, hands in pockets, glumly beginning his long walk home. As the Porsche's throaty exhaust surged he looked up; his eyes met mine and I waved at him – not a proper wave, because Simon would have noticed that, just a little flutter of my fingers.

But Brad saw me. Oh, yes, he did. I saw the startled look in his eyes, the way he suddenly stood upright as if he'd been slapped.

Simon didn't even notice as I smiled to myself. It serves Brad right, I thought; if he's seeing someone else, so am I. With bells on!

The heady elation lasted all the way home. When Simon stopped at my house, he got out of the car to open the door for me.

"I'm sorry we couldn't make a night of it," he said, "but duty calls. Maybe we should meet up later?"

I thought, how dare you assume that's what I want! But I just meekly said "Goodnight" and I ran into the house.

Maddie was in the living-room, watching a film on Sky. "You're late," she said.

"My boss took us out to dinner," I replied.

She shrugged and went back to the film and I went upstairs to bed. It was too late to make myself sick and besides, for once, I didn't want to.

Just for once, I wanted the dream to last, but I'd

take an extra dose of laxatives tomorrow anyway.

It was only when I lay in bed thinking that I remembered that tomorrow was the day of Brad's interview.

Chapter 14

I felt awful about it the next day, of course. In fact, I felt awful about it immediately. I tossed and turned that night, but there was nothing I could do. I decided to phone Brad in the morning, but I fell asleep when dawn was breaking and when I woke up, late, his mother told me that he'd already left for his interview.

I didn't leave a message.

I hated myself so much that, at lunchtime I went home and took the emetic. I wanted to punish myself. When I dragged myself back to Breeze, I looked so awful that Carin sent me straight back home again. She didn't say anything about Simon, though I'd told her that nothing had happened.

Alone in the house, my self-hatred burgeoned into an overwhelming force. I began to eat, and when I'd finished the contents of the fridge, I opened the freezer and began to gnaw at a frozen cheesecake. When that was finished I started on a quiche. I ate so much frozen food that eventually I was sick naturally.

Afterwards, I began to write a letter:

Dear Brad,

I'm really sorry, you don't know how sorry. Afterwards I couldn't believe what I'd done. I didn't mean it. The man I was with is my boss; he flirts with me, but no more than that. I know you won't forgive me but I just wanted to tell you anyway. You see, Naomi saw you with another girl, and I was really upset about that. I wanted to get even, that's all. It sounds silly, doesn't it?

I know it's over between us now, but I really didn't mean to hurt you and I hope I didn't. You're right, I am obsessed with my weight. But, you see, I've been dieting forever and I just never seem to lose any. I'm still fat. The thing is, it's a vicious circle, because I know you wouldn't love me if I'm fat, and then when I tried to be thin you didn't love me because of that. I always thought you'd really love me when I'm thin, but I don't suppose I'll ever know because I'll never be thin. It's my body – there's something wrong with it; there's something wrong with me. I stay fat whatever I eat. I look fat, I feel fat, I am fat. And there's nothing I can do about it, although I have to try, because I just can't bear it to be like this. For once in my life, I want to be thin. That's not a crime, is it?

I really, truly didn't mean to hurt you. Please try to forgive me although, if you can't, I quite understand. I'm such a horrible person, I don't deserve someone like you. But it was nice for a while, because I really thought I could change.

I'm so sorry, Brad. If you can't forgive me, please try not to hate me too much.

That letter was the first of many. Of course, I didn't post any of them. For the first time in my life, I seriously began to think about suicide. I didn't know what to do, but there were some sleeping pills in the medicine chest because Mum always gets jet lag when she comes back from the States, and I thought that would be a start, with some alcohol of some sort. Maybe that would give me the courage to slit my wrists.

Something always stopped me. At first, it was the thought of what it would do to Maddie if she found me, because even though she nagged me and at times I hated her, I didn't want to do that to her. And then it was a little glimmer of sanity that told me that my life hadn't always been like this, that maybe it wouldn't be this way for ever more.

But beyond that, I still felt a desperate compulsion to lose weight. It was so strong that nothing else mattered in comparison, not Brad and not suicide, because if I did kill myself I'd never know whether I could actually do it or not.

It was very strange, the way that with all this inner turmoil I managed to go on as normal. I went to work and talked to people, I came home and cooked meals. I even ate them sometimes, although afterwards I purged myself. Maddie was my albatross; I thought that when she was gone, I could maybe deal with Mum and Dad, although when Gran came back in October I'd be in trouble again.

I became so devious that Maddie didn't stand a chance. I got my ski thermals out and took to wearing them underneath my clothes so that she couldn't see my body contours; I made myself salads with beans on top and only celery underneath; I ate so much celery that she never noticed that I left the beans.

Celery is a truly great diet food! In fact, I don't know if "food" is the right word for it because it's only got eight calories in a hundred grams.

My parents were away in Indonesia for two and a half weeks. Towards the end of that time, all my deceptions paid off at last because Maddie announced that she was going to Paris for the weekend to be with Christian. I was looking forward to the prospect of some time alone.

Late on Saturday afternoon, Simon came into the shop again. Carin wasn't there, because her sister was visiting; there was only us three assistants, with Lallie in charge. Breeze was having a fashion show in September and he asked us to put on some of the clothes that he wanted to show then.

It was the first time I'd seen him since he'd taken me home and I just didn't know how to react to him. In my mind, Simon was like double chocolate cheesecake, enticing but also dangerous. Although I liked hearing the things he said to me, I was never sure that he was telling the truth.

"Why did you run away from me the other night?" he asked as I drifted past in the latest from Milan.

I stiffened; he just had that effect on me. "I didn't. I was tired, that's all."

"Did I really bore you so much?"

"You didn't bore me at all."

"Good," he said.

Naomi gave me one of her homicidal stares as she walked out of the changing room wearing a leather trouser suit. His eyes stayed on me, not her.

That spell wound its way around me again; that luxurious illusion that I was thin and not at all repulsive to look at. For a moment I hovered on its edge, then I tumbled into it.

"You look delicious," Simon said, as if he could see straight into my head. He glanced at his watch. "Why don't you all come to the club tonight?"

"I'm busy," I said.

"Cancel it. I'll pick you up at eight o'clock."

He walked out without waiting for a reply. The silence he left in his wake was heavy, like lead.

"I'm not going," I said.

Lallie shrugged. "It's usually pretty cool at the club."

The girl who worked on Saturdays said she'd come too.

Naomi's eyes were sparking with envy.

"OK, I'll go," I said.

If she was jealous, it served her right.

Simon picked me up first. When he saw me, he smiled slowly, his eyes travelling over me like twin electron microscopes. I flushed; although the dress I was wearing was nice, it was nothing like the clothes in Breeze.

He reached into the back seat and handed me a carrier bag. "Do me a favour," he said, "wear this instead."

I hesitated, then I went inside and changed into an outrageously expensive Japanese dress. I sat in the front seat of the car; Lallie and the other girl had to squeeze into the back.

The club was empty when we got there; Simon ordered some champagne and then left us at a table. I'd never been in a club before, but it was just like I expected, all dark and glittery with soft lighting on the tables and music that throbbed like an adrenalin rush. As I watched, the room began to fill up slowly; girls came in in twos and threes, their lurid make-up softened by the lighting as they scanned the room like predators. Boys, or maybe I should say men, came too, but they clustered at the bar clannishly.

I didn't touch the champagne; when a waiter

passed, I asked for a mineral water. After a while, I went to the loo, where the bright lights blinded me after the gloom of the club. There was something about the place that I didn't like. I was thinking about Brad, wondering if he'd got through the interview OK, if he ever thought of me at all these days. It had been more than a week since I'd seen him, and my heart ached with regret at what I'd done. There was a sudden commotion outside, the sound of male voices, then the door opened and Lallie came in.

"What's going on?" I asked her.

"It's the rowing club's end-of-summer party. All blokes and no girls. That must've been why Simon invited us, to make up the numbers for the boys." Nonchalantly, she began to redo her make-up.

Anger rose inside me. I walked out and went to the cloakroom, where I collected my jacket, then I headed straight for the door. Just before I reached it, I felt a hand on my arm.

"You're not leaving?" Simon said.

I glared at him. "Of course I am. I'm not going to be free entertainment for your rowing friends."

His grip tightened. "Jo, that's not why I asked you here tonight."

I made a futile attempt to shrug him off "No?"

"No. I wanted to see you, but I was afraid you wouldn't come if I asked you alone." He grinned sheepishly. "Please don't go. At least, let me talk to you for a while."

I shrugged. When he smiled that way, he looked

like a little boy. He opened a door in a corridor and led me up some stairs to another door, which he opened with a key. It led to a room overlooking the river that glowed golden in the light of the setting sun, punctuated by the inky silhouettes of the trees on the banks.

"I don't like your club much anyway," I said.

He smiled. "This isn't my club, it's the place where I live. Don't you like the view?"

I ignored it and looked around. The floor was pale blonde wood, a deep leather sofa was set in front of an unlit fire. There were pictures on the walls; Andy Warhol's stylized image of Marilyn Monroe repeated endlessly in technicolor.

Simon flicked a switch and the fire was lit; it was gas, not real coal. "Just one drink," he said, as he took a bottle of champagne from a fridge set into the wall. The champagne fizzed as he poured it into glasses. He handed me one, then sat down on the sofa opposite me.

I sipped a little.

"I really like you, Jo," he said.

I was thinking how I'd lost Brad, the boy I loved.

"You're perfect, d'you know that?"

I shook my head vigorously.

"That's what's so perfect about you," he said, "you don't know it. You're not vain. You're honest. You're a real person." He shrugged. "The others, they're clones. They're trying to be this actress or that model, they want to be anyone but themselves. But you, you're real, Jo. You're an original. Maybe you don't know it yet, but soon you will."

I trembled inside and took another sip of champagne to steady myself. Once again, there was warfare in my head, between the part of me that could not believe him and the other part, which said that a man like him wouldn't say something like that if it wasn't true. I was just so low, so depressed with everything that, even though I didn't like him, I really liked what he said.

I took yet another sip of champagne and relaxed as its warmth spread through my body. I hardly noticed when Simon refilled my glass.

"You don't believe me," he said in that low, throaty voice of his, "but you could be a model — really you could. I've a friend in London who's a photographer; I could get him to take your picture if you like."

I thought about it, not trembling because the champagne anaesthesia had taken effect by then.

"You don't think I'm too fat?"

"Nnooo," he said, thoughtfully.

"I mean, aren't my legs lumpy?"

"I don't think so. I haven't seen all of them."

"And I'm not neurotic? I'm not crazy about dieting?"

"Jo! You're the sanest person I know."

I drank champagne as I thought about it.

"You really are beautiful," he said, as he refilled my glass. "Your body is flawless. *Flawless.*"

I drifted away on that dream-like word as his face closed over mine and he kissed me deeply. I was dizzy, not with him but with the revelation that all my dieting had worked at last. My mind was spinning with the realization that I might find happiness at last. I wasn't aware of what Simon was doing until I felt his hand on my breast as his hot breath puffed against my throat.

I drifted for a moment longer and then I remembered that, if I wanted anyone to make love to me, I wanted it to be Brad. If my body was good enough, I wanted to share it with him and not with this man who held such a strange blend of attraction and repulsion for me.

As Simon's other hand drifted lower, I realized that I didn't want him at all, I only wanted to hear the nice things that he said to me.

They're not true!, the voice roared inside my head, *He's only saying them to get you into bed!*

I tried to push him away but the champagne had weakened me; I was dizzy as well and at first he took it as a come on.

"Oh Babes!" he exhaled.

That was it. Reality hit me like an icy-cold shower. I shoved him off and then ran for it. I forgot about the sandals that had slipped off my feet but on the way out of his flat I managed to grab my jacket. As I raced helter-skelter down the stairs, his voice followed me:

"That's my dress!" he roared.

Once I got out of the club I ran along the road for a bit, stopping when the pain in my feet overwhelmed me.

The effort had exhausted me; needles of agony

lanced my muscles. I breathed deeply as the cold night air drove the last of the champagne out of my system. I was only a little way out of town, but the road was quiet and there were no cabs. Although I had a jacket on, the diaphanous dress was just a whisper against the wind.

I shivered and began to cry. I was so ashamed of myself that I wanted to die. I'd hurt the boy I loved and then let the local wise guy treat me like a slapper. I just didn't deserve to live.

Numbly, I trudged on into town. When I saw the hospital looming in front of me, I scuttled down a back street, afraid that I'd bump into Brad. It was just after eleven, and he would be leaving work.

I decided to write to him, and this time I *would* post the letter. After all, I owed him an explanation, and whatever he thought or did when he read it wouldn't hurt me, because by then I'd've killed myself.

Beyond the hospital, I headed home, wandering what combination of pills and alcohol would be enough.

Then I heard steps behind me. "Jo?"

I turned round. It was Brad. He took one look at me, then he put his arms around me and hugged me. "Who did this to you?" he asked.

I looked down at my feet, scratched and torn by the road. The Japanese designer dress now looked like a reject from the Oxfam Shop. "I'll tell you the whole story some time," I said, "but the real answer is, I did it to myself."

Epilogue

We talked right through the night. I can't remember exactly what I said, I only know that I wasn't making a lot of sense. In the morning, we went to my doctor. I was admitted to hospital immediately because, by then, I'd lost over thirty per cent of my body weight.

I hadn't realized how ill I was, or, before Brad found me that night, that I was ill at all. I was pretty dopey for the first few days as I was drip-fed sugar and the nutrients I'd been starving my body of. As I began to recover, the doctor explained that I had eaten so little that I had inflicted serious damage on myself. Luckily, I got help just in time; in my case the damage was not permanent.

My parents came home from their holiday early. There were no recriminations; they were terribly concerned. I discovered the hard way that they loved me, not my idea of who they thought I was.

Poor Maddie was beside herself. She thought it was all her fault, that she should have done something sooner, but the truth was that she had no idea of how bad things really were because I'd become so good at hiding it.

They all spent a lot of time blaming themselves, but I'd been so devious, there was nobody to blame apart from myself. I felt awful once I realized what I'd put them through, but when you have an eating disorder, you're blind to the consequences – you're blind to everything except your own distorted vision of yourself.

After I was discharged from hospital, I spent three months in a clinic being treated for my eating disorder. Nobody called it anorexia at first, but that was what it was, if you have to put a name to it. I kept denying it, but eventually, with a lot of help, I began to realize what had happened to me – and how serious it was. Ten per cent of people with an eating disorder die, by suicide or the effects of starvation. So if you're ever thinking about dieting when everyone around tells you that you're already thin, think twice.

I'm one of the lucky ones. I recovered, or, at least, I'm in the process of recovering. Although nearly two years have passed, I'm still not sure I'm over it.

There's nothing wrong with wanting to be thin, but when dieting takes over your life, it's time to stop.

As I write these words, a lot of things have changed in my life. I missed a lot of school, and when I went back, I no longer had the same compulsion to get perfect marks. Through counselling, I'd realized that I was driving myself too hard, trying to become someone that I was not. We all did. Mum and Dad came to counselling too. We all changed; we spend more time together and we laugh a lot; our lives aren't as pressured as they once were.

Though they both still work very hard, we finally had our swimming-pool put in last year and they both take time in the summer to enjoy it.

I still don't know what I want to do with my life, but I know I have plenty of time to decide. I haven't seen Naomi since that last day at Breeze; I've made new friends, friends that I trust.

One thing didn't change. As I began to recover, my love for Brad came back to me, stronger than it had been before.

He got on to the pilots' training scheme. Part of the course was in Australia, so he couldn't come to see me, but he wrote funny letters full of jokes.

I missed him so much! I was sure that it was over between us. I'd put him through a lot of misery, more so because of what he had already gone through with his sister.

The question was never, would he love me when I was thin? but rather, why wouldn't I let him love me the way I was? When I think back, it's so clear that's what he wanted to do, but I was so blinded by my obsession that I didn't realize that.

When he got back from Australia, I was out of the clinic, although I was still going to counselling three times a week. He came to see me the day that he got back. We were really nervous with each other at first, and then I took a deep breath and told him how much he meant to me.

Through counselling, I have learned not to play games with people I care about. I also gained the courage to be able to be honest about myself. I had nothing to lose but my pride, after all; if I'd lost Brad, nothing that I could say would make any difference to that.

Brad gazed at me for a long time, and then he said, "I love you too, Jo."

So, that's it for the moment. We're still together. (When he saw me naked, he didn't go "yuk!")

I don't know if it will last for ever, but I do know that we've been together for more than two years now, and it just keeps on getting better and better.

Brad's just started as a First Officer on short haul flights. I'm doing a language course part-time, and I also spend a couple of days a week counselling people who are going through the same thing that I once did. My life is moving on, becoming richer.

I only know this: for Brad and me, even for ever would not be long enough.

If you or anyone you know is suffering from an eating disorder, you can contact the Eating Disorders Association at the following address:

1st Floor
Wensum House
103 Prince of Wales Road
Norwich
Norfolk
NR1 1DW

or ring their youth helpline on 01603 765050 (Mon. to Fri. 4 to 6 p.m.).

"He loved drugs more than me"

"Want some?" said Kieran, breaking the spell of the quiet that had been between us. I looked round, expecting to see him holding out a stick of chewing gum or something. Instead, I saw that he was holding out a small white pill, smaller than a paracetamol or an aspirin.

"What is it?" I asked.

"It's an E. Ecstasy. You want a bit?"

Ecstasy? Kieran was offering me *drugs*? I mean, there'd been that time when Rory had tried to pass me a joint, and Kieran had taken him up on it – that had shaken me up enough. But this was different. Ecstasy was *really* serious stuff. I'd no idea he was into it. I couldn't take it in. This couldn't be for real – it couldn't be true. I didn't want anything to spoil this amazing time we'd spent together, I didn't want it sullied with anything like this. I didn't know what to say, so I said something stupid.

"You're kidding!"

Kieran burst out laughing. I felt like crying. Was he laughing at me, my naïveté?

"Oh Alice, you're so sweet!" he smiled, then looked at me with eyes full of concern. "What's your problem with it?"

What was my problem? It was a full-on, scary, proper drug, that's what the problem was. The TV news spoke about teenagers dying on it, the local papers went on about there being an epidemic of it in our area, and as a result the headmaster gave us endless lectures about avoiding it. That's what the problem was. And up until a minute ago I'd felt warm and happy, knowing that the only thing that would make me even happier was if Kieran had leaned over and kissed me. But now that moment was ruined. *That* was my problem too.

All that went on in my head, but what came out of my mouth was something idiotic and un-expected.

"I – I've never tried it."

"Tell me something I don't know," he laughed. I shuddered a little, unnerved. Maybe I *had* been naïve, maybe this *was* what everyone was into and I'd just never realized. Did Joe and Aaron take it and I just never knew? How could you spot some-one on E?

"Alice, I wouldn't let you try anything that you wouldn't like, would I?" His pale grey eyes stared earnestly into mine. "It'll just make you feel really relaxed and happy."

"I feel relaxed and happy now," I argued lamely.

"You don't have to take a whole one, just a little bit. Just a quarter."

Just a quarter? Just a quarter of that tiny white pill? The bigger part of me, the part that wouldn't touch cigarettes or alcohol, wanted to smile politely and say no to Kieran. The smaller part of me, the part that was fascinated by this skinny boy with the beautiful face, wanted to trust everything and anything he said.

"OK," said a voice I didn't recognize – the small part of me speaking out before the sensible part got a word in edgeways.

"Good on you, Alice!" said Kieran, breaking the chalky pill into first half, and then quarters. I took the tiny piece he held out to me, my hand trembling.

"Go on," he encouraged me, smiling broadly. I felt like he was somehow proud of me for doing it.

Before I could change my mind, I threw the thing into in my mouth, swallowing it back with a gulp from the small plastic bottle of water Kieran passed to me.

A noise like thunder filled my ears. It was the sound of my heart beating frantically with agitation and anticipation, drowning out the far-away music, the birds singing in the tree above me and the voice of reason shouting "no!" at the back of my mind.